CITY OF PREY

(An Ava Gold Mystery—Book One)

BLAKE PIERCE

Blake Pierce

Blake Pierce is the USA Today bestselling author of the RILEY PAGE mystery series, which includes seventeen books. Blake Pierce is also the author of the MACKENZIE WHITE mystery series, comprising fourteen books; of the AVERY BLACK mystery series, comprising six books; of the KERI LOCKE mystery series, comprising five books; of the MAKING OF RILEY PAIGE mystery series, comprising six books; of the KATE WISE mystery series, comprising seven books; of the CHLOE FINE psychological suspense mystery, comprising six books; of the JESSIE HUNT psychological suspense thriller series, comprising nineteen books; of the AU PAIR psychological suspense thriller series, comprising three books; of the ZOE PRIME mystery series, comprising six books; of the ADELE SHARP mystery series, comprising thirteen books; of the EUROPEAN VOYAGE cozy mystery series, comprising six books (and counting); of the new LAURA FROST FBI suspense thriller, comprising five books (and counting); of the new ELLA DARK FBI suspense thriller, comprising six books (and counting); of the A YEAR IN EUROPE cozy mystery series, comprising nine books (and counting); of the AVA GOLD mystery series, comprising three books (and counting); and of the RACHEL GIFT mystery series, comprising three books (and counting).

An avid reader and lifelong fan of the mystery and thriller genres, Blake loves to hear from you, so please feel free to visit www.blakepierceauthor.com to learn more and stay in touch.

ISBN: 978-1-0943-7481-9

BOOKS BY BLAKE PIERCE

RACHEL GIFT MYSTERY SERIES
HER LAST WISH (Book #1)
HER LAST CHANCE (Book #2)
HER LAST HOPE (Book #3)

AVA GOLD MYSTERY SERIES
CITY OF PREY (Book #1)
CITY OF FEAR (Book #2)
CITY OF BONES (Book #3)

A YEAR IN EUROPE
A MURDER IN PARIS (Book #1)
DEATH IN FLORENCE (Book #2)
VENGEANCE IN VIENNA (Book #3)
A FATALITY IN SPAIN (Book #4)
SCANDAL IN LONDON (Book #5)
AN IMPOSTOR IN DUBLIN (Book #6)
SEDUCTION IN BORDEAUX (Book #7)
JEALOUSY IN SWITZERLAND (Book #8)
A DEBACLE IN PRAGUE (Book #9)

ELLA DARK FBI SUSPENSE THRILLER
GIRL, ALONE (Book #1)
GIRL, TAKEN (Book #2)
GIRL, HUNTED (Book #3)
GIRL, SILENCED (Book #4)
GIRL, VANISHED (Book 5)
GIRL ERASED (Book #6)

LAURA FROST FBI SUSPENSE THRILLER
ALREADY GONE (Book #1)
ALREADY SEEN (Book #2)
ALREADY TRAPPED (Book #3)
ALREADY MISSING (Book #4)
ALREADY DEAD (Book #5)

THE PERFECT SMILE (Book #4)
THE PERFECT LIE (Book #5)
THE PERFECT LOOK (Book #6)
THE PERFECT AFFAIR (Book #7)
THE PERFECT ALIBI (Book #8)
THE PERFECT NEIGHBOR (Book #9)
THE PERFECT DISGUISE (Book #10)
THE PERFECT SECRET (Book #11)
THE PERFECT FAÇADE (Book #12)
THE PERFECT IMPRESSION (Book #13)
THE PERFECT DECEIT (Book #14)
THE PERFECT MISTRESS (Book #15)
THE PERFECT IMAGE (Book #16)
THE PERFECT VEIL (Book #17)
THE PERFECT INDISCRETION (Book #18)
THE PERFECT RUMOR (Book #19)

CHLOE FINE PSYCHOLOGICAL SUSPENSE SERIES
NEXT DOOR (Book #1)
A NEIGHBOR'S LIE (Book #2)
CUL DE SAC (Book #3)
SILENT NEIGHBOR (Book #4)
HOMECOMING (Book #5)
TINTED WINDOWS (Book #6)

KATE WISE MYSTERY SERIES
IF SHE KNEW (Book #1)
IF SHE SAW (Book #2)
IF SHE RAN (Book #3)
IF SHE HID (Book #4)
IF SHE FLED (Book #5)
IF SHE FEARED (Book #6)
IF SHE HEARD (Book #7)

THE MAKING OF RILEY PAIGE SERIES
WATCHING (Book #1)
WAITING (Book #2)
LURING (Book #3)
TAKING (Book #4)
STALKING (Book #5)

KILLING (Book #6)

RILEY PAIGE MYSTERY SERIES
ONCE GONE (Book #1)
ONCE TAKEN (Book #2)
ONCE CRAVED (Book #3)
ONCE LURED (Book #4)
ONCE HUNTED (Book #5)
ONCE PINED (Book #6)
ONCE FORSAKEN (Book #7)
ONCE COLD (Book #8)
ONCE STALKED (Book #9)
ONCE LOST (Book #10)
ONCE BURIED (Book #11)
ONCE BOUND (Book #12)
ONCE TRAPPED (Book #13)
ONCE DORMANT (Book #14)
ONCE SHUNNED (Book #15)
ONCE MISSED (Book #16)
ONCE CHOSEN (Book #17)

MACKENZIE WHITE MYSTERY SERIES
BEFORE HE KILLS (Book #1)
BEFORE HE SEES (Book #2)
BEFORE HE COVETS (Book #3)
BEFORE HE TAKES (Book #4)
BEFORE HE NEEDS (Book #5)
BEFORE HE FEELS (Book #6)
BEFORE HE SINS (Book #7)
BEFORE HE HUNTS (Book #8)
BEFORE HE PREYS (Book #9)
BEFORE HE LONGS (Book #10)
BEFORE HE LAPSES (Book #11)
BEFORE HE ENVIES (Book #12)
BEFORE HE STALKS (Book #13)
BEFORE HE HARMS (Book #14)

AVERY BLACK MYSTERY SERIES
CAUSE TO KILL (Book #1)
CAUSE TO RUN (Book #2)

CAUSE TO HIDE (Book #3)
CAUSE TO FEAR (Book #4)
CAUSE TO SAVE (Book #5)
CAUSE TO DREAD (Book #6)

KERI LOCKE MYSTERY SERIES
A TRACE OF DEATH (Book #1)
A TRACE OF MURDER (Book #2)
A TRACE OF VICE (Book #3)
A TRACE OF CRIME (Book #4)
A TRACE OF HOPE (Book #5)

CHAPTER ONE

New York City
August 1928

The cheering, screaming, and applauding were getting to him. The sidewalks were filled with rowdy people attending a political rally and march—and they were almost all women, to his disgust. Once women had somehow achieved the right to vote, they seemed to think that meant they had to go out and make spectacles of themselves. There were songs and shouts, cheers and whooping. Among it all, he could see signs made of newsprint and plywood. Many of them said the same thing: **Vote SMITH for a Stronger USA!**

He'd been on the way to the baker's, but the noise in the streets was jarring and the further away from his house he got, the worse the noise became. He'd turned back, feeling the yelling and singing behind him like a wave pushing him back to shore. He could get bread tomorrow. It wasn't like he had a family depending on him back at home.

There was no wife waiting with a warm meal in the afternoon, no kid to beg for attention and time. There was only his ailing mother, not really ill but certainly mentally unbalanced—always wailing and screeching at him, wanting to know why he was always struggling to make ends meet, wanting to know why he hadn't married a nice young woman to start making her some grandbabies.

Feeling the thoughts of his mother growing like some raging wind, he pushed them away and focused on his walk. It was six in the evening, the day creeping toward dusk. And though the heat of the day was now dwindling, he felt the headache coming on. Maybe it was the roaring of the crowds, an unfamiliar noise in the streets he called home. Maybe it was the tension of knowing what awaited him at home. Whatever it was, the headache was coming on fast, starting at his jaw, working through his teeth, and reaching up into his skull.

After what felt like forever, he arrived home. It was a simple two-bedroom house located in a section of the city that was not the poorest, but far from the wealthiest.

He closed the door and the crowd noises were little more than a murmur. He stood there for a moment, his fingertips pressed to the door. The house always had a sort of dusty smell with an underlying note of vegetables just on the brink of going rotten. It greeted him like an unwanted embrace as he turned away from the door.

"What the hell are you doing?" the old, ragged voice from the living room asked him.

He looked to the right, and there was his mother. She was sitting in the same chair she always sat in. Over the past year and a half or so, as his mother had given up on any hope of remarrying or starting up a social life after the loss of her husband, he'd watched the empty space of that chair shrink by the week. His mother had put on at least eighty pounds in the last eighteen months, eating cakes and pastries he often brought back from the city.

"Nothing," he said, finally stepping away from the front door.

"You go out to whoop and holler with all those uppity whores?" she asked.

He noted crumbs in the folds of her shirt and something that might have been jelly in the corner of her mouth. He also noted that her eyes showed that same level of disappointment and anger as she looked at him. Beyond it all, there was the vibrating hum of the political march in the streets and as he stood there, looking at her and listening to that quiet noise, he understood why the sounds of the women's shouts had unnerved him.

It was her. At some point after losing so many jobs and unable to attract a girlfriend, she had become the embodiment of all women to him. Always leering, always wanting something more from him, always disappointed.

"What the hell are you staring at me like that for, you simp?" she asked. "Get your useless backside in the kitchen and bring me my brandy."

The headache roared in his head. It was like a bomb, sending little shards of shrapnel into every corner of his skull. He sucked in a breath, chewing back the pain.

"Get it yourself, you cow."

Her look of shock was mostly muted by the chunkiness of her cheeks and her squinting little eyes. "What did you say to me?"

"You heard me, Mother."

He walked away from her, fully intending to go to his bedroom and lie down in the darkness. With her eyes on him and with the thrum of marching and yelling outside, he felt his headache getting even worse. If he could rest in a dark room, maybe the throbbing would lessen.

Her voice stopped him as he walked away. "Your father thought he knew what was best for me, too," she said. "But look which one of us is still alive. Now fetch me my brandy, you useless idiot."

The headache surged once more, slamming around in his head like a wrecking ball. Black spots filled his vision and something like black curtains waved at the edges of his sight. He grimaced against it and sucked in a lungful of stagnant air. Through clenched teeth, he said: "Yes, Mother."

He walked down the small hall, his feet treading the old, creaking floorboards. He entered the kitchen but did not stop at the cupboard where his mother stored her brandy. He moved as if pushed by some unseen force, perhaps by the outside screaming of the countless women on the streets. Without even thinking about it, he walked to the back door and opened it. He stepped out onto the back stoop, just a single concrete block that looked out onto their mostly dead back yard.

He closed his eyes, the headache digging into his skull like railroad spikes. He could hear the cheering and laughter in the streets, a million women it seemed, all either encouraging him to do what he was about to do or laughing at him because he was so damned powerless in the presence of his mother.

To the right, there was a small stack of rotted wood they used to occasionally fill the old, almost-defunct fireplace in the living room. Propped next to the house was the hatchet he used to split the wood. It was old and dull and he could remember being a boy, his father teaching him how to shave off kindling and how to find the crack in the top of a piece of wood that would make it easier to split.

He grabbed the hatchet and walked back inside—back through the kitchen, back down the hallway. It pleased him in an odd and almost poetic way to know that the creaks of the hallway floor would be among the last noises his mother would ever hear.

The creaking of the floor seemed to thrum with his headache. Somewhere very far away, he could hear the cheering of all of those women, their long hair warming in the sun, their taunting bodies sweating and forbidden.

The last creak before arriving in the living room, everything went dark as the headache slammed down an iron curtain over his sight and senses.

Moments later, he dropped the hatchet and headed back out through the front door.

Covered in blood, he walked toward the sound of the cheerful women. With each step he took, his headache faded and the joyful sounds swallowed him up, bloodstains and all.

CHAPTER TWO

New York City
July 1929

Her husband was dead, resting in the casket just three feet in front of her, and all Ava Gold could think was that there was an abundance of hats filling the small club during the wake. Men and women alike, both civilians and police, were wearing hats of varying shapes and sizes. It was sunny and bright outside, a gorgeous day ruined by having to lay her thirty-four-year-old husband to rest, and all of the hats around her reminded her of beach umbrellas she often saw out on Coney Island. Strange, she thought, how the brain does everything in its power to distract from the reality of death.

Currently, her brain was trying to comprehend the idea that she was going to have to live the remainder of her life without her husband. She knew it was the truth but it did not seem real. She went over the facts in her head time and time again, as if repeating the words to a song she'd sung hundreds of times: her husband, Clarence Gold, shot five times while responding to a basic robbery call. The suspect had been wearing a thick workman's coat, was relatively short—and that's all she knew. That was all the details the witnesses had been able to provide.

She had not expected so many policemen to attend the wake, but they had come out in droves. Their uniforms almost tying the entire scene together as if they had stitched the moment themselves. In about five minutes, they'd all relocate to the cemetery, and she supposed it would be the same. Hats and policemen, swarming her like bees.

Even now, as their church pastor was reading from Psalms, she was dimly aware of a policeman giving an encouraging pat on the shoulder to her son. Jeffrey, sitting to her left and staring at the casket as if it were a problem to be solved, seemed not to notice. Ava knew how he felt and wished she could explain it. She'd done her best over the three previous days but she had come to the conclusion that it was impossible to process grief with a nine-year-old when your brain refused to accept the reality of the situation. Jeffery had not said much of anything since his father had died. At the age of nine, she supposed death was a tricky beast indeed. You were too young to fully grasp the finality of it, but old enough to understand that there was pain there, and you were expected to respond a certain way.

Ava was bookended on her right by her father, a man she usually drew comfort from. Now, though, she saw him as a man who was simply there, another face in a crowd there to her mourn the loss of her husband. Ava figured there might be more of a connection between them if her father had spent more time with her when she'd been young rather than in a boxing ring. She'd always felt guilty about savoring the night he'd come home with a shattered left hand; she'd known even then it meant the end of his boxing career. Now, Roosevelt Burr, who had chosen a boxing ring over his family, mourned another man who had chosen a career over family.

The pastor wrapped up his reading, said a prayer that Ava barely paid attention to. Some took it as a signal to come by and say "hello" or "sorry for your loss" or "he's in a better place now."

And then everyone was excused. As the ranks of policemen started to file out of the club and to the Model Ts that would take them to the cemetery, someone started playing a trumpet out on the front lawn. As the tune to "Blessed Assurance" filled the front room of the club in thin brassy tones, Ava caught a glimpse of something that felt familiar and whole—something that helped to remind her that yes, she was attending her husband's wake and yes, it was all real. The sound of the trumpet, even as flat and boring as the hymn currently made it, never failed to lift her spirits. As she got to her feet and took Jeffrey's hand, Ava thought of ways the trumpeter could improve it. A run here, a hook there, and then she could sling some voice to it.

Jazz, she thought to herself. *You're really thinking of jazz in this moment?*

She felt her father's strong hand on her arm, leading her forward. Apparently, she'd stopped walking. It was the grief, she supposed. She felt it building within her and knew that at some point the dam would break and she'd lose her mind. She wanted to look back to the casket, but did not dare.

"Ava?" a man's voice said.

She blinked like she'd just come out of a nap and looked to her right. She recognized the face as that of Captain Douglas Minard. He had a kind face that was rudely being overtaken by age. He was nearing sixty but his life experience made him looked closer to eighty. He took her small hand in his large, calloused one. When he looked at her, she appreciated the fact that he had been crying; his eyes were red and the streaks of tears were evident around them.

"Captain," she said. "Thank you so much for coming."

"Of course. I wanted you to know what a great deal I thought of Clarence. He was one of the best...in and outside of the department. And oh, how he loved you and bragged about you."

Ava smiled warmly, wondering if Captain Minard was trying to get her to cry—for that tension inside of her to snap.

"Yes, he was. He was my..."

But she could not find the right words. Every time she'd tried to describe him in the past three days, she'd felt like an idiot. It was as if her vocabulary had shriveled up and died, each loving word that described Clarence rotting on the trembling floor of her mind.

"Ava...is there anything at all that I or anyone at the department can do for you?"

Her tongue formed the word *no* but her brain overruled it at the last moment. Looking at Captain Minard, she wondered if the answers to a prayer she'd been sending up ever since Clarence's death was in the process of being answered. And when the next four words came out of her mouth, they shocked her. She couldn't help but wonder if Clarence was here, somehow, perhaps possessing her from the afterlife.

"I'd like a job."

"A job?" Minard asked, clearly stunned. Had he not been crying previously, she thought he might have laughed at the comment.

"I need to support Jeffrey. And I want to stop the next son of a bitch from turning a child into an orphan...a wife into a widow."

Captain Minard looked around at everyone else as they filed out, as if for a life raft out of this strange situation. He also noted Ava's father standing about three feet away, making no attempt to hide the fact that he was listening in.

"Ava, perhaps this is your grief talking," Minard said, his voice low. "Surely you don't want a job with the police. Besides being a woman, the sort of people you'll have to deal with are—"

"And what's wrong with being a woman?" Ava asked. She was nearly *hoping* he'd make some ignorant comment about how women were not cut out for police work.

"Nothing. But you can't..." He stopped here, stumped. She almost felt bad for putting him in the situation but he had, after all, asked.

"I will not just sit aside while my husband has been blown down," she added, surprised at how confident she sounded.

"Ava, you can't just…I mean, we have plenty of capable men to find killers and—"

"Then where is my husband's killer?"

Minard looked as if he'd been slapped across the face. And was that a flicker of anger she saw? Apparently, the truth hurt. Four men had seen her husband shot; four men had seen the man who had pulled the trigger. Yet his killer remained at large. Minard looked over to her father, still looking for a way out of this, but Rosie Burr only shrugged and smiled.

"You're a singer, correct?" Minard asked. "A rather good singer from what I hear. Why not stick to jazz? Why not—"

"I'm more than a canary," Ava interrupted. "Dames can pull a trigger just like a man." She was getting irritated and welcomed it. She'd rather be mad than saddened in this moment. This anger might be what got her through the graveside service without crumbling into a sobbing mess.

She took a step closer to Minard, trying to remain polite and respectful but firm at the same time. "Clarence once told me that the men he worked with were like a family. That they were like brothers. He told me that if anything ever happened to him, his brothers would have my back. And now, here I am answering your question honestly. Can you do anything for me? Yes: you can get me a job as a detective."

Minard took two steps away from her, realizing that he was still holding her hand. He released it slowly and looked around the room. The trumpet still played outside, and the front room was empty except for Ava, Captain Minard, Roosevelt Burr, and Clarence Gold's casket. Jeffrey had apparently been ushered out by one of Clarence's friends. Noting this, Minard worked some bass into his voice. Any semblance of sorrow or sympathy started to dissolve.

"Okay, Ava," he said. "I will see what I can do. But I can tell you right away that you will not make detective. It's just not a place for women. Whatever job I can land you…"

He paused here, looking to Ava's father. Minard had surely heard of Rosie Burr's boxing days and was choosing his words carefully.

"Any job I can get you won't have room for advancement, but it will be a steady paycheck. Come to the office on Monday and I'll get you squared away."

She managed a nod because she was afraid to say anything else. It felt like a victory, sure, but it also felt like some high-rolling egg had called her bluff. And in an even odder way, she felt it was the first thing she'd done since Clarence had been blown down that he would be proud of her for.

"Thank you," Ava said, not breaking eye contact.

Captain Minard turned away and took a few steps toward the door before stopping and turning back to her. "I'm glad your father was here to hear this. That way, I can't be blamed when you start having problems. And you *will* have them. Most women don't last more than two weeks."

With that, Minard walked out the door in the direction of the trumpet's dull tones.

Rosie chuckled and put an arm around his daughter.

"What's funny?" Ava asked.

"Most women don't last two weeks," Rosie said, quoting Minard. "Damn shame for him that you aren't 'most women,' huh?"

She smiled but for some reason, the comment brought on tears and she felt that tension inside of her about to break. With her head down and resting on her father's shoulder, Ava Gold walked outside and tried to find some groove to that sorrowful old trumpet as she prepared to bury her husband.

CHAPTER THREE

Ava looked at the 37th Precinct from across the street. For just a moment, it was like peering into some other land, some fantastical place she'd only ever heard of. It was a grand-looking building, just a design choice or two away from looking elegant. It stood out easily as the premier building within a few blocks, as if a beacon to remind criminals this was where they'd end up.

A sting of nervous excitement rampaged through her as she crossed the street. She was so distracted that she nearly stepped right out in front of a Model T. The driver bellowed something about a "crazy dame," shaking his fist as the car puttered by. It was almost as if she'd filtered out the outside world—that, for a second or two, the entire world had consisted of only her and the 37th Precinct.

Six days had passed since Clarence's funeral. It didn't seem like enough time to have passed to carry on, to start this new chapter of her life. But at the same time, those six days felt like an eternity. Besides…Clarence would not want her sitting around weeping over him. She felt that she was doing the right thing, without a doubt.

When she walked inside, it was a bit staggering. There was a large open space and people milling around behind desks and what she assumed was the "bullpen" she'd heard Clarence refer to a few times. She approached the front desk and looked to the pale, overweight man sitting behind it.

He regarded Ava with a smile that seemed authentic. "Help you?" he asked.

"Yes, my name is Ava Gold. I have an appointment with…well, I'm not sure with who. But Captain Minard is expecting me."

At the mention of her name, understanding dawned in his eyes. "Ah yeah, of course. Been expecting you." He picked up the receiver on the in-house phone on his desk. He pressed a button as if he were stabbing someone and waited a beat. He then spoke two words into the mouthpiece: "She's here."

Neither of them said a word and as a handful of seconds passed, Ava became aware of other men looking at her as they passed by, going about their morning duties. Some were not eyeing her as an insect like the hefty man was, but more like a juicy piece of steak to be devoured.

Less than a minute later, a middle-aged man came walking quickly through the bullpen toward the front desk. His eyes locked directly on Ava and he walked as if he were in a hurry. A mostly gray moustache covered his upper lip and he wore glasses that made his brown eyes seem to sparkle.

"Mrs. Gold?" the mustached man asked.

"Yes."

"Good to meet ya," he said. He impulsively seemed to want to offer his hand for a shake but then apparently decided it might not be proper. "I'm Wayne Gibb and I have the pleasure of showing you around. It's not an orientation, but it's the best we got." He offered a shaky smile and then waved her on. "Follow me."

Gibb opened the little swinging door that led behind the bullpen. When Ava walked through, she was pretty sure everyone in the station stopped breathing for a moment. It was eerily quiet and she could *feel* their stares on her. She supposed she understood it—but that didn't make it right. The passing of the Nineteenth Amendment had not changed nearly as much as people wanted to believe it did. Yes, women could vote, but they were also still seen as nothing more than living, breathing units to keep homes tidy for their husbands; they were expected to clean and cook and spit out a baby whenever their husbands thought the timing was practical.

She did her best to look past this as Gibb walked her through the precinct. She'd heard Clarence talk about it countless times but to see it up close was dreamlike. She saw all of the offices and hallways, the rogues' gallery on the far right wall by a group of desks she assumed were taken by detectives. She saw signs indicating the direction of the mailroom, the holding cells, and even the small gymnasium—which she knew, thanks to Clarence, was often used to store prisoners captured late at night so they could be photographed and profiled in the morning She wished she could get poetic and misty-eyed by realizing she was walking the same halls Clarence had once occupied, but she didn't. She wasn't *dare* going to cry in front of these men who were already betting on her to fail.

"You, of course, will be placed with the Women's Bureau," Gibb said. "There's a nice bunch of dames in the bureau that will get you worked in to everything."

She had several questions about the Women's Bureau, but she did not want to seem too eager or ill-informed so she stayed quiet. She followed Gibb and listened to his lackluster tour of the precinct: breakroom, restrooms, bullpen, location of the in-house phones that connected all of the offices, armory, and the location of the Women's Bureau. She was not all that surprised to find that it was located near the back of the building. It was also down a small flight of stairs, as if making sure the women knew they weren't *actually* part of the club upstairs.

As she and Gibb walked along, she saw many men starting at her. Some gave sly little smiles. It all made her wonder if they simply didn't care that they'd spent several years working with her husband—getting to know him and respect him. Did all of that vanish just because she'd had the audacity to assume she could work here? She wondered if Gibb knew. She assumed he did if Minard had assigned him to her. She wasn't sure if she appreciated the fact that Gibb had not mentioned it or if it angered her.

"There will be some paperwork, of course," Gibb said as they came to the bottom of the stairs that led to the Women's Bureau. "But we'll get that all to you by the end of the day. Any questions?"

She had many but didn't want to seem foolish, so she simply asked the most pressing one. "Is there some sort of training program?"

Gibb shrugged, and Ava could also see that he was doing his best to suppress a smile. "You're about to get it. You've been assigned to partner with a current woman in the bureau. She'll show you the ropes."

They came to the end of the hallway, where a set of double doors sat in the wall. A sign hung from the doorframe that read NYPDWB. *As if the situation itself wasn't awkward enough,* Ava thought, *even the abbreviation is awkward.*

Gibb opened the door but did not step inside. He gave a smile and said, "If you have any questions, any of these ladies should be able to answer them. If not, you can come back up to the front and ask for me."

"Thank you," Ava said.

And with that, Ava walked into the room and took the first step on the path she was determined would become a career.

***

Almost instantly, it was clear that these women—fourteen in all—knew that no one took them seriously and they took it with something like honor. They were all cordial, though there was something different about all of them. Ava could tell that much without even speaking to any of them.

12

A short woman with broad shoulders met her as she stepped in through the door. She had a homely face but her hair looked as if it was taken excellent care of. It bobbed slightly above her shoulders when she walked over to Ava.

"Gold, right?" the woman asked.

"Yes, that's right. Ava Gold."

"Ava, my name is Frances Knight. I'll be overseeing you until you get your feet under you. I've been here from the start—which isn't long, let me tell you—and I know just about everything there is to know about the WB—the Women's Bureau."

Before Ava could say a word, Frances Knight placed a hand to her back and led her across the room. As they walked side by side, Ava realized that she was easily eight inches taller than Frances. She took a look around the room and noted very quickly that this place, in comparison to the rest of the building, was little more than a slightly remodeled basement.

"Your desk is here," Frances said, nodding to a desk that sat like driftwood in front of them. "And no, we can't move it."

The desk was an ancient beast of a thing, pushed into the corner. It was so old and scarred that Ava could easily imagine portions of the Constitution had been penned on it. A stack of papers sat on it, along with two brand new pens.

"Standard protocol says you have to read all of those documents," Frances said. "There's no tests or training or reciting afterwards. You just have to sign a paper that says you read it all and understand it."

"Okay…"

"Now, if you'll excuse me, I need to get back to this report I'm working on. Let me know if you have any questions."

Frances spoke fast and by the time she started making her way back across the room, Ava felt as if she'd just survived a hurricane. Ava looked around the room as she took her seat and saw that a few of the women were looking at her. She also noticed that only a few of them wore makeup of any kind and their hairstyles were plain and drab for the most part. There were nine women currently in the room, but fourteen desks. Of those nine women, three were looking at her curiously, and another with something like worry.

Ava looked away, focusing on the papers in front of her. She started reading them and was surprised at how much of the verbiage in them reminded her of conversations she'd had with Clarence about his work. There were details on proper investigative procedures, but it was very brief. She wondered how heavily edited the documents had been for the WB as opposed to the men upstairs.

About twenty minutes into her studying, she came to a set of documents detailing what her behavior and attire should be like. Some of it made her cringe. It was written in a way that almost sounded as if the women working at the 37th Precinct were little more than pets.

As she read over the *Proper Attire for Women* guidelines, a thin woman with a sharp chin leaned down over her shoulder. "The best thing to do with that information," this woman said, "is take it home and use it for toilet paper. No matter what you wear around here, the men are still going to stare at you. And believe me, honey, it ain't flattering."

"What they *really* can't stand," chirped another woman at a desk nearby, "is when you forget to wear a brassiere."

There was an outburst of laughter at this but as soon as it was started, it died down. A few of the women looked guilty for enjoying themselves and looked directly back at the files and paperwork on their desk.

The tall, sharp-chinned gal sighed. "That," she said, "is called laughter. You don't hear much of it down here in the WB. Women, if you didn't know, are to be seen, not heard…Nineteenth Amendment be damned."

"I sort of hoped it would be different here," Ava said.

"It can be, from time to time." The woman then did something Ava had never seen a woman do; she offered her hand to be shaken, as if they were two men sitting down to have a chat. "The name's Lottie Mattingly," she said.

"Ava Gold," Ava responded, taking the woman's hand and shaking it. Lottie's grip was firm and tight. Ava decided that she liked Lottie Mattingly right away.

"You know, some of us crossed paths with your husband from time to time," Lottie said. "He was a damned fine man. He was one of the few that didn't mind working with us. We were fellow detectives to him, not just broads." She frowned and added: "I'm so sorry for your loss."

"Thank you. He was—"

She was interrupted by a loud blaring noise. It took her a moment to realize that it was the phone. Ava had never heard one so loud. It rattled and rang like an alarm. She noticed that even some of the regulars jumped a bit, clutching their chests and letting out nervous laughter.

Ava looked around the room as the phone rang a second time. At the other end of the room, Frances was muttering a string of curses under her breath as she got up from her desk, pen in hand, and walked to the house phone installed on the cinderblock wall.

"This is Knight," Frances announced into the phone. Ava noted that she held the receiver end of the phone to her head as if she did not trust it—like it might be a loaded gun rather than a phone. "Yes, sir," Frances said, nodding as she followed the conversation. "Yes, sir. Of course…Are you sure? Yes, I'm sorry, of course. Yes, sir."

Frances placed the receiver back on the phone cradle and sighed. She regarded the room, shaking her head. Very quietly, she said: "What a bunch of dull saps."

"What is it?" one of the women asked. Ava saw that they were all looking at Frances with something close to anticipation. It made Ava think they didn't often get calls from the men upstairs.

Frances looked directly over to Ava and sighed. "You about done with those papers?"

"Nearly. Why?"

"Skip ahead quick and sign," Frances said. "I just got a direct order from Captain Minard. He wants me to take you out on patrol."

There was a flurry of conversation among the women. Some sounded nearly entertained while others were clearly aghast. Ava noticed that a few were giving her looks of pity, as if she were a calf about to be led to the slaughterhouse.

"But that makes no sense," Ava said. "I haven't even been here for two hours."

"Don't I know it," Frances said.

"He's trying to prove a point," Lottie said from her desk. "He wants you scared. He wants you doubting yourself."

It took Ava a while to put the pieces together and when she did, she was both angry and embarrassed. "So you all know…?"

"That you asked him for a job at Clarence's wake?" Lottie said. "Yeah, we know. And no one here judges you. If I could rub out the coward that killed him, I'd do it. I can only imagine how you feel."

"In other words," Frances said, tossing her pen on her desk in frustration, "be ready in five. You and I are about to hit the streets."

***

Having no idea that she'd be on patrol on her first day, Ava had dressed modestly but professionally. The purple day dress had been a favorite of Clarence's so it only seemed fitting. The dress was fine in terms of walking a patrol route, but the flapper-style pumps were going to cause roaring hell on her feet within a few hours. After only the first block, she made a mental note to get better walking shoes.

She also took note of the streets themselves. Walking down the street at this time of the day was a stark reminder that the city now contained nearly six million people, and the place seemed to grow every day. It smelled of cologne, perfume, and a slight tinge of liquor from where the prohibitionist police force had recently been dumping liquor into the gutters. And though she'd gotten somewhat used to the looming presence of the newly created skyscrapers, she couldn't help but feel like an ant in the midst of it all.

"Oh, this is for you," Frances said as they hurried along a crosswalk. She handed Ava a small whistle with a chain around it. "Wear it around your neck, and blow on it if you see something that needs the attention of the police."

"But aren't we the police?" Ava said.

"We are. But we're women. We see crimes, we blow the whistle, and the men come running."

A familiar flash of anger and resentment rose up in Ava. She had ever done very well at accepting a woman's second-class position in the world. "Doesn't that allow the criminals time to escape?"

"It does, and it's a foolish way to go about the job. But it's..." Frances paused when they came to the next street and pulled Ava to the side. "Listen to me. This is very much a man's world. Always has, always will be. If you wanted this job thinking that there was equality within the police, you may as well pack it up and go home now. Don't get me wrong...it can be rewarding and can put deserving women in the spotlight for a day or so. And every now and then, who knows? Maybe you even get to take part in something exciting. But for the most part...this is it. Walking a beat and looking innocent and of no importance. It stinks, but it's also genius. Most men that are capable of committing crimes see us and we're just two random broads. And with you...well, they see a dish. They'd never expect that you were a flattie."

"Flattie?"

"It's what some of these cretins on the streets call the coppers."

"Oh."

"So, you just keep looking pretty and keep that whistle hidden under that dress. And speaking of that dress, it seems you really need to pay more attention to those What to Wear guidelines."

In Frances's typical hurricane style, she started walking the moment the last word passed her lips. Without turning to face Ava, she kept on talking. Ava could tell the woman liked her job and that she wanted other women to do well. She was the sort of woman who had accepted that women were seen as subservient and not only embraced it, but seemed to use it to her advantage.

"Unless something big changes," Frances was saying, "your patrols will keep you around Morningside Heights and Harlem. Low crime rates and an easy beat. You might see minor robberies or bickering as men leave for work. But that's about it. Now, if you—"

Frances was interrupted by a man who passed by them. A devilish grin was plastered on his face as he said, "Hey there, sweet thing. Let me see how long those gams are!" He chuckled as he kept walking in the other direction.

"And you may as well get used to that, too," Frances said. "Now, let's be real. Have a look at me. Take a gander. I don't get many remarks like that. But some of the other girls do. And there's not much you can do about it. You'll get a badge at some point, but most men don't give a damn about that."

"Would they give a damn if I decked them in the mouth?"

"Maybe," Frances said, smiling. "But that's a surefire way to lose your job. I do like the fighting spirit, though. That come from being married to Clarence?"

"And having a boxer as a father. I used to spar with him from time to time."

"Actual boxing?"

"Yes," Ava said, trying not to sound too proud.

"Good to know. I'll do my best to stay on your good side."

They walked on, continuing the route as Frances spoke at length about what to expect. She told Ava that for the most part, the WB didn't venture into harder neighborhoods like the Lower East Side or the Italian Quarter. "That's where a lot of those mobster shitheads hang out," Frances explained. "Not the best place for a woman—even if she does have boxing experience. Don't get me wrong…things can get seedy around here, too. Prostitution is a growing problem and speakeasies keep popping up all over the place. So keep your eyes open for that sort of thing. And hey, it's pretty easy—look for women dressed like tramps and men that are red in the face and are having trouble walking."

It was odd, but with each block they passed and with more information from Frances, Ava started to feel more comfortable with the job—day dress and flapper pumps aside. A big part of it was the pride and excitement for the job Frances carried; she was so happy to be showing her around, to bring another woman into the WB. While Ava still absolutely felt like the new, inexperienced broad on the block, she was already starting to feel a sense of pride about what this job could mean.

The morning wore on and the summer heat managed to stay somewhat hospitable. It had been a mostly cool summer, which she assumed meant August and September were going to be sweltering. She wasn't sure how far she and Frances had walked by the time her feet *really* started to yell at her, though she guessed it was about a mile and a half or so.

"I'm so sorry," Ava said. "I need to stop for just a moment. These damned shoes…"

"No problem. I really wish someone would have given you a heads-up on what you'd be going through today. Walking a beat in those shoes has to be torture You got different shoes at home?"

"Yes," Ava said, leaning against the side of a butcher shop. She slipped off her right pump and allowed her foot to breathe. "A nice pair of flat-footed Mary Janes that—"

A woman's yell from behind them cut her off. "Hey! Someone, stop him! *Thief!*"

Ava and Frances turned in that direction just in time to see a teenage boy rushing toward them. His eyes were staring dead ahead as he clutched a small purse to his chest. He was wearing a newsboy-style cap, pulled down low on his head. Ava saw Frances go for her whistle but the teen was too fast. He passed by Ava, apparently assuming her leaning stance against the butcher shop was out of fear and letting him pass by. He then threw a hard shoulder into Frances's chest, sending her stumbling back against the building. The sight of it sent a spike of adrenaline into Ava and she started after him with one shoe still removed. She balled her hands into fists, recalling the lessons her father had given her. She was right-handed, but she figured she'd start with a left-handed jab when she caught up to him, shocking him just enough to sneak that devastating right hook across his jaw.

But within three striding steps, Ava stopped. She recalled what Frances had said earlier, about how giving chase or attacking a criminal could result in being reprimanded or even losing her job—a job she hadn't even been at for an entire day.

But at the same time, there was a sense of justice crawling up from deep within her. It told her there was no way in hell Clarence would approve of her just laying low and blowing on a whistle. With the adrenaline and anger now taking the controls, Ava removed her other shoe, tossed them in Frances's direction, and went running.

Almost as if it were a sign of some sort, Ava passed by a store that was playing jazz music. She could barely hear it, but the bass line and wailing trumpets seemed to encourage her. She ran down the block, attracting the attention of every single person she saw. She pulled her whistle out from beneath the top of her dress. She placed it into her mouth and blew. It was much louder than she'd expected and it seemed to rattle the insides of her head. As she blew on it a second time, she realized that Frances was staggering behind her, shouting out warnings to her. Ava knew she was already breaking a lot of rules but it was too late now. She was running after the thief and he was within her sights. She figured at some point, the whistle might clue in another copper, and they'd nab the guy.

And if not—if she reached the young thief before a man could come to the rescue—then she'd just have to tackle him. Oops…maybe she tripped and fell on him or something.

Ava bounded through the thin crowd of people along 101st Street, blowing her whistle a third time. She wasn't even sure how far she'd run, blowing the damned whistle. Three blocks? Four?

It then occurred to her that blowing the whistle was counterproductive. It was alerting the thief to where she was. And while she knew her only job was to blow on the damned thing until a male cop showed up, she found the idea not only stupid, but antiquated. She released the whistle from her lips and let it drop to her chest.

She came to the end of the block where the purse-snatcher had taken a left. It was here that Ava saw a thin alleyway that ran between a little candy store and a grains and tobacco shop. It was mostly opened, blocked only by a few crates and trashcans. Ava halted, the bottoms of her stockinged feet scraping on the sidewalk, and went rushing through the alleyway. She knew it would come at just shy of the end of the block and she'd make it there before the thief because he was having to contend with pedestrian traffic and she was not. She leaped over a crate, feeling the grit and overall sliminess of the alley against her stockinged feet. Still, she ran hard—the whistle forgotten, protocol forgotten, even Frances partially forgotten.

Ava came to the end of the alleyway and looked to the right. She saw a few people stepping aside in a hurry and knew why right away. She dashed in that direction and saw the thief coming through the crowd of people. She then put her whistle back into her mouth, waited for him to get closer, and then blew hard on it.

The sound, up so close, shocked him. As Ava advanced, she saw that he nearly dropped the purse. He then turned and headed back the way he had come. He glanced back over his shoulder a single time, his eyes wide with fear now, and that's when he ran directly into the arms of another cop. This was a policeman of about six foot seven, with shoulders like slabs of granite. The thief rebounded a bit but was snagged by the cop. The thief was pushed against the wall of the sundry shop the policeman had just come out of, and as the policeman handcuffed him, there was a confused buzz coming from the passing pedestrians.

The cop pressed the thief against the wall and then looked at Ava. His eyes narrowed and he shook his head as if he were about to admonish a stubborn dog. "What the hell do you think you're doing?" he barked at her.

"Chasing a thief," Ava answered without much thought.

"And causing a scene! You were supposed to blow on your whistle and nothing more."

"I did! I'm sure you heard it. But if I hadn't chased him down—"

But the cop was already looking away from her. Ava wanted to keep arguing her point but knew it was useless. That little defeat allowed her to come down out of the adrenaline of the moment and when she did, she realized that she *had* overstepped. She should have listened to Frances She should have—

"Gold?"

Ava looked around and saw Frances coming out of the alleyway. She was huffing for breath and looking at her with an odd mix of satisfaction and anger. She hurried over to Ava, shaking her head in the same way the cop had.

"You left these," Frances said, handing Ava her shoes. "Also…what the hell were you thinking?"

"I'm sorry. I just…I couldn't just let him run off while I stood there blowing my dumb whistle."

"Blowing that dumb whistle is your job. Running down hoods is not."

There were several things Ava wanted to say but she kept her mouth closed. It was her first day on the job and she'd already broken several rules. She watched as the cop started hauling the thief away. He gave no thank-you and didn't even bother looking back to scowl at her again. As far as the cop was concerned, she'd done nothing but break rules.

"I like you, Gold," Frances said. "But if you want to make it in this job, you have to suck it up and do what you're told. And please, for the love of God, don't ever do anything like that again."

Ava said nothing. She gave her anger a moment to subside by putting her shoes back on. When she and Frances started to walk, continuing their patrol, she tried to process it all. And though she knew it had been her whistle that had alerted the cops, Ava still felt like she had failed somehow. And if this had been her first day, it made her wonder what tomorrow would bring.

CHAPTER FOUR

Roosevelt's Boxing Club was slow and quiet when Ava walked inside. There was a rapid-fire beat coming from the back as someone was working on the speed bags. Though Ava's feet were sore and it had been a demoralizing day, it all washed away when she took in the familiar sights and smells of the small gym space.

There were also several punching bags in the back, along with some second-rate strength-building equipment. Two men were sparring in one of the rings with a coach looking on. The man running speed drills on one of the bags in the back was being overseen by her father, watching with his arms crossed and a steely look on his face.

She saw that the man at the speed bag was a little off on his timing. His wrists were locking a bit on each punch as he waited for the little bag to come back to him. She approached timidly, watching with the same intense gaze as her father. When Roosevelt Burr saw his daughter, he smiled warmly and patted the trainee on the shoulder.

"Take a second, would ya?" Roosevelt told the man. He was a younger guy, likely in his early twenties. He nodded, sweat dropping from his messy hair.

Roosevelt looked from Ava to the speed bag and said, "Wanna show him how it's done?"

She did…quite badly, in fact. But she also just wanted to pick up Jeffrey and get home. She could come down sometime over the weekend and work the bags—maybe even get in a bit of sparring. There were a few regulars to her father's club who would still work with Ava in the ring, though there was a larger number that wouldn't. She'd been throwing gloves in those things for the better part of ten years now and had taken at least a dozen men to their limit, cake-eaters and brunos alike. The men at the 37th Precinct might not know how tough she was—how excellent of a fighter she was—but just about every man who had ever stepped foot into Roosevelt's Boxing sure as hell knew.

"No thanks," she said. "It was a hell of a day and I'd really like to just get home. There is, of course, the matter of my son."

Roosevelt chuckled. "He's in the back, lacing up some of the older gloves."

"I'm glad you put him to work."

"You know, he's like lightning on the bags, too. Not nearly as good as you but...with time who knows?"

Ava started for the back but her ears were still tuned in to the sparring match taking place in the ring behind her. She could hear the patter of footwork, the slapping of glove against glove, glove against body. In an odd way, it was just like the jazz music she'd grown to love and become slightly obsessed with. There was intricacy to it, a beat to follow, but also a lot of improvisation. Maybe that's why the two things—boxing and jazz—had always appealed to her.

She found Jeffrey in the small equipment room. He was busy lacing up a pair of well-worn gloves. There were a few other pairs already laced to his right.

"So Grandpa put you to work, I see," Ava said.

"Yeah, a little. But he let me play in the rings. And he let me hit the bags!"

"So I heard. You about ready to get home?"

Jeffrey nodded as he finished lacing up the gloves. He set them aside and came directly to Ava for a hug. It was tight and he buried his head in her shoulder. This was something new—something he'd only started doing since the funeral. She did not mind it at all, though she did wish he would openly talk about how he felt. His insistence on keeping all emotion shoved down deep was something he'd gotten from her so she understood it.

They walked back out into the workout room where the men in the ring had stopped sparring. Back at the bags, the sweaty young man had gone back to hitting the speedbags. Roosevelt was walking across the room to meet them, leaning down to give Jeffrey a hug goodbye.

"You guys okay?" he asked, looking up from his hugging stance at Ava.

"Yes, Dad. We're good. I just...I need to be home. It's..."

What she almost said was *"it's the only place I really feel him anymore"* but decided not to. She knew her father had instantly stepped up, wanting to fill the role of a strong father figure in Jeffrey's life. She didn't want him thinking she was on the verge of becoming a huge, sobbing mess.

"You need me to watch him tomorrow?" Roosevelt asked. "He fits in well around here, you know."

"Tomorrow *and* Friday if that's okay. I'll figure out some other solution soon, but right now—"

"Don't be silly," Roosevelt said. "I love having him here. He's welcome to stay here anytime you need."

"I don't know about Jeffrey being around all of this," she said.

"And why not?" Roosevelt asked with mock hurt in his voice. "You were around it quite a bit from what I remember. And you turned out pretty damned good." He then looked down to his grandson and said, "Did you know your mom used to spar with me and some of the chaps around here?"

"What?" Jeffrey asked, his eyes wide. He looked to Ava as if he were meeting her for the first time.

"Thanks for that, Dad," she said with a smile. "Now get back there to your student. And for the love of God, tell him to loosen up his wrists."

Roosevelt gave her a quick hug and then did just that. Ava then led Jeffrey out of the boxing club and out onto the streets that she was now being paid to help protect.

They walked home in mostly silence as Jeffrey made little boxing motions, his fists balled up and his eyes narrowed. It was only a three-block walk, but Ava's feet were good and tired by the time they made it home.

Home was a small apartment that she'd always been afraid she and Clarence could not afford. But they'd made it by just fine because of Clarence's thrifty habits. Now, with him gone, the apartment seemed too big and reminded her of just how important it was that she keep this job. If she kept chasing down hoods and ignoring rules and protocols, they could lose their home.

They were both tired—Ava from her first day on the beat and Jeffrey from his manual labor at the boxing club with his grandfather— so bedtime came quickly. Ava was still not used to getting Jeffrey into bed by herself. Clarence had usually played at least some part in it, even if it had been simply making jokes or playfully wrestling the boy into bed.

"Why didn't you tell me you were a boxer?" Jeffrey asked as she settled him down into bed. The question came at Ava like a bullet from a gun; it was a topic that seemed almost dangerous now. She was now the only parent and the way her son saw her seemed more important than ever.

"I wasn't a boxer," she said. "I just spent a lot of time at the boxing club right after your grandfather stopped boxing. I even went with him when he trained when he was still fighting from time to time. I practiced with him and after a while, I got pretty good."

"Are ladies even allowed in the boxing clubs?" Jeffrey asked.

"Not most of them. But your grandpa doesn't mind."

"And you fought men?"

"I *sparred* with men. There's a difference."

"Yeah, but did you beat them?"

Ava smiled. "Yes, I did. Now…no more about that. You need to get to sleep if you're going to help Grandpa again tomorrow."

Jeffrey accepted defeat and laid his head down on his pillow. His room was small but tidy, like most of the other rooms in their rather drab apartment. They had never wanted for anything, but neither she nor Clarence were the sort to spend money just for the sake of spending it.

"Can you tell me a story?" Jeffrey asked.

It was another question that stung. Clarence had always been in charge of bedtime stories. His stories had been filled with daring adventures of heroic detectives, often taking place on the streets Jeffrey saw every day. As a mother, she wanted to be able to tell such stories to her boy, but her heart tightened like a safe in her chest when she thought of even trying.

Rather than answer outright, Ava sat in bed beside where Jeffrey lay and tousled his hair. "You know how you told me a few days ago that you aren't ready to talk about how you feel now that your father is gone? That you weren't even sure what you'd say."

Jeffrey nodded. He wouldn't look at her for a while, though he did reach out and take her hand.

"Just like you, there are some things I need to think about…some things I need to get used to. Do you understand?"

Again, all she got was a nod.

"Well, as much as I hate to say no to you over something like this, I can't stand to even try to tell a bedtime story. I think I can sometime…and probably pretty soon. But right now, so soon after he's been taken from us, I think it would hurt too much. Do you understand that?"

This time when he nodded, a tear slipped out of Jeffrey's left eye and trailed down his cheek. "Do you miss him?" Jeffrey asked.

"I do," Ava said. "Every single second of the day."

"Was it neat to be where he used to work today?" Jeffrey asked.

"You know, that's not an easy question to answer." She sighed and leaned over to Jeffrey, kissing him on the forehead. "I love you, Jeffrey."

"Love you, too." He shifted under the covers to get comfortable but Ava didn't get up.

Instead, she sat there for a while, listening to her son's breathing as he fell asleep. What she'd almost told her father was the truth: their apartment was the only place she truly felt Clarence anymore. But it was also sort of like walking through a tomb. Because it was more than just bedtime stories. It was the living room, the kitchen, the bedroom and their marriage bed. Everything in her life felt so much emptier without Clarence.

And for now, there was only her and Jeffrey to fill these spaces. She had some Clarence-sized spaces to fill in the coming weeks, months, and years—bedtime stories being only one of those things. She thought deep down, that might be why she'd asked for the job at the precinct. It was another way to keep Clarence close and to bring something into her life that had been a huge part of his life.

She wept quietly for him as Jeffrey fell asleep beside her. And later, when she also fell asleep in Jeffrey's bed, one of the final things that went through her head was the sight of the young thief from today…of how she'd had to restrain herself, blowing into that stupid whistle for some man to come and save the day.

And what the hell sort of bedtime story would that make, anyway?

Still, the apartment was quiet and the longing she felt for Clarence was like drowning. But this apartment was hers now. She and Clarence had lived and loved here, had raised their son here. And if bowing to protocol and sexist rules was what it was going to take to ensure that they kept it, she'd do her best. Tomorrow was a new day, and she promised herself (and, to some degree, Jeffrey) that she'd do whatever she could to make sure she played by the rules from here on out.

CHAPTER FIVE

Ava had not been at her desk for five minutes before Frances was there, looking down at her with pity.

"I see you wore some sensible shoes today," Frances said.

Ava looked down at her walkers and nodded. "Just in case."

"Well, it was a smart decision. You and I just pulled patrol duty for the entire day."

"All day?" she asked.

"Yes, the entire shift. We'll of course get a lunch break, but other than that, you and I are on the streets."

Ava looked to her desk and processed it all. She supposed it made sense to push her right away—for Minard to make good on the little veiled threat he'd made at Clarence's wake. Not only had she asked for this, but she'd asked for it knowing she'd be standing in the rather defined shadow her husband had left on the 37th Precinct. That, plus the fact that she was a woman, made it appear as if the entire situation had been engineered to fail.

"Get yourself set up here and meet me out in the front lobby in fifteen minutes. Maybe grab a coffee, too. It's going to be a long day."

Ava nodded as Frances went back to her own desk to prepare for the day. She then slowly pushed away the *Proper Arrest Protocol* document she'd been reading and sat in silence for a moment, trying to center herself before getting upset with Minard and those above her who seemed to want her running away in fear.

The moment didn't last long, though. Lottie walked over with a knowing smile on her face. Ava was starting to understand that Lottie was something of a pot-stirrer—the sort of jane who always had something to say about any authority passed down that she did not like. Ava wondered if she'd been one of those very vocal ladies who had raised enough hell to finally get the Nineteenth Amendment passed a decade ago.

"Hey, it could be worse," Lottie said. "You could be paired up with me. I tend to draw attention to myself when I'm on the beat."

"Oh, you can't be that bad," Ava said. "Not any worse than what I did yesterday, anyway."

"Oh yeah, about that," Lottie said. "What the blazes were you even thinking?"

"I suppose I wasn't."

"That's for sure," said another of the women. She was a tall, waifish-looking doll named Myra. She was pretty, but knew it a little too well, which made her a little *less* pretty. "You got guts on you, that's for sure. But the coppers…they don't like women with guts."

"Even if we're on the same team?" Ava asked.

"But we aren't on the same team," Frances said. "We might be in the same building, but you see where they put us, right? Bottom floor. Away from the actual police work."

"Don't get us wrong," Lottie said. "You're a firecracker, that's for sure. And we like you. So please…keep yourself in check. Another outburst like yesterday and you're outta here."

"Sad but true," Frances said.

"We're all rooting for you," Myra said, batting her overdone eyelashes.

"She's right," Lottie said. "The entire precinct lost a good man when Clarence died. I figure he rubbed off on you, and maybe you on him too. Either way, it's good to know he's sort of still around."

Lottie gave a quick wink and then went back to her desk. Ava then saw Frances grab her whistle from her desk drawer, placing it around her neck. Not seeing the point in delaying the inevitable, Ava also grabbed her whistle. She understood that being on the street all day was going to be rigorous and tiring, but she did prefer that thought over sitting behind a desk all day and sifting through paperwork.

"Ready?" Frances asked as she caught Ava walking toward the door.

"I really think I am," Ava said, trying on a smile that almost felt genuine.

***

They headed out and this time Frances headed to the west, toward a stretch of the city they'd barely even touched on the day before. Ava knew it well; it was just on the cusp of Harlem, where she had sung with a few different jazz ensembles. It had caused quite a stir, a white woman singing with a jazz outfit of mostly black musicians. But racism, as far as Ava was concerned, was just as stupid as sexism. Singing in some of those clubs was among the best experiences she'd had. And the few times she'd visited the Cotton Club as a spectator had been instrumental in her love for jazz and the passion that would keep her singing for several years.

Within three blocks, she could hear the thumping of a bass and the wailing of a saxophone. She knew it was just musicians warming up, as it was far too early for any actual shows. Still, it made her feel comfortable, more at home.

"I heard you used to be a singer, right?" Frances asked.

"I still am," Ava said. "Whenever I get the chance. Some musicians used to call me—pianists, usually. But the calls stopped coming. Some folks didn't take kindly to me singing with a black band."

Frances shrugged. "I get sort of spaced out on the music, you know? I come here sometimes just to unwind. And because it's on my patrol beat, I'm not breaking any rules. Sometimes I'll find one of these little jazz holes and perch myself right outside, having a listen. White…black…I don't care if you're green. If you can play music like this, who gives a damn what color you are?"

They walked slowly through the area, coming into Harlem and passing another little club where someone was rolling through soundcheck. Someone was playing a few notes from the chorus section of "Downhearted Blues" by Bessie Smith. Ava found herself humming along, nearly forgetting that she was working at all—until they came across a shouting match on the corner.

Ava did her best to quickly dissect the situation. A shoeshine boy that was calling the customer every name in the book. They had not yet gotten too loud, but it was going to cause quite the spectacle within a few moments.

"What's the matter here?" Frances asked.

"Shithead owes me a nickel, is what!"

"Not for this wretched job!" the customer moaned.

Ava wasn't sure how to break such an argument up. Would the customer—a handsome banker-looking type—even take the authority of a female police officer seriously? She watched Frances, eager to learn the ropes.

Frances took a look at the shoes and then looked up at the man. "Not like mirrors by any means, but they look clean enough. You really going to make yourself look like a fool over a nickel?"

"This boy needs to learn the honor of hard work! A lazy job won't get him anywhere."

"Nor will arguing with a child right here in public will get *you* anywhere. That suit jacket you're wearing…how much you pay for that?"

"Well, that's none of your business."

"Give the boy his nickel. Don't be an ass."

The man looked to the whistle on her neck and Ava saw when he rolled his eyes. He recognized her as a cop, sure, but the roll of the eyes indicated that to him, they were no more than silly dames playing dress-up.

The man pulled a nickel from his pocket and flicked it at the boy. The boy, agile and quick, snatched it right out of the air and gave the banker-type a big grin. "Thanks, *mister*."

The man eyed the female detectives one last time and then stormed off.

"Gee, thanks, Officers," the boy said.

Frances beamed at him and then hunkered down to look into his eyes. "No problem. By the way, those shoes looked like holy hell. Start doing a better job if you expect people to pay you."

And with that, they were off. Frances said nothing about the moment while Ava played it back in her head, noting how Frances had dealt with the boy and the man in different ways—in ways they'd understand and almost appreciate.

Maybe it was the little trek through the outskirts of Harlem or the growing trust and familiarity with Frances—whatever it was, the afternoon went by quickly and smoothly. Her feet were hurting again despite the proper footwear but Ava figured all of the walking would at least help her keep in shape.

About half an hour after the incident with the two boys, Frances checked her watch and tapped it. "Time to head back. I'd say that was a decent day's patrol, how about you?"

"I don't know. How often do you have to patrol all day?"

"Maybe once a week. We usually break it into shifts. Again...I think this might be some sort of fear tactic. And for what it's worth, I hope it's not working."

They headed back down the same blocks as dusk started to fall. It was broken just as they passed back by the little jazz clubs. The soundchecks had come to an end; Ava figured the musicians might be elsewhere, sneaking a few illegal drinks to juice up for the night's shows. She recalled the blissful nervousness of performing but did not have time to dive deep into those memories.

Instead, her concentration was broken by the sound of a terrible scream. Ava had never heard anything like it. But still, she recognized it as a sound of fear and pain, a wretched sound that sent a chill through her heart.

Both women went running toward the sound as it belted out again. This time, there was pain in it. Also, it was acute enough for them to pinpoint the exact location. It was an alley that ran between an apartment building and one of the small jazz clubs. For Ava, there was no question; she took off running down the alley to help in any way she could. And though she sensed the hesitation in Frances, she also came running up behind her, unable to match Ava's speed.

Ava had made it just five or six steps into the alley when she saw a fallen figure on the ground and another figure standing above the body. The standing figure had something in its hand—a large hatchet from the looks of it—and was raising it into the air. Ava's heart and gut worked together and made a judgment call in that moment. She knew she was far faster than Frances and she should go after the standing figure, even if it was to chase him toward a larger crowd by blowing her stupid whistle.

Fleeting thoughts of the warnings Frances, Myra, and Lottie had given her flashed through her head but she killed them off right away.

She dashed after him without thinking. It was an act that surprised the man. He hesitated, the hatchet raised mid-swing. He then turned and ran. It was, Ava knew, a mistake. She was lightning fast and even though he had a weapon, she'd catch him. She knew this was not the man who had killed Clarence, but it was a man who had hurt a woman and left her for dead—a man who thought it was okay to act in such a way. That was enough motivation for her.

She faintly heard Frances protesting behind her. "Dammit, Ava!"

The man with the hatchet came to the end of the alley and turned right. Ava did the same, her eyes focused on the man's back. He was leading her through a series of back alleys which she knew, deep down, might even be some sort of a trap. These were likely alleys he knew well and Lord only knew what sort of people slunk about here. Even now, as she watched the man shoulder down another thin alleyway to the left, Ava was quite sure she passed by the back of a poorly disguised speakeasy.

Ava went down the same alleyway and saw the man weaving his way through a fractured wooden fence that ran along between two brick buildings. The alley was no more than four feet across, making it a tight fit. The attacker had to squeeze, sucking his gut in to pass through. He still held the hatchet and even in the shadow of the alleyway, she could see blood smeared all over the blade. He was still struggling with the fence when she made it halfway down the alley. When he did finally clear it, she did not lose heart. She was far slimmer than he was and she would be able to—

A man appeared as if out of nowhere to her right. He came lumbering out a small doorway to what must have been another speakeasy. Even in the split second she clearly saw his face, Ava could tell he was intoxicated. She could smell hard liquor on him as he reached a hand out and punched her in the chest.

Ava stumbled backwards, the wind rushing out of her. She fell against the side of the wall and the man fell against her. One hand held a knife. The other groped her right breast with a violent sort of need. "You see this blade?" he said. "If you don't let *me* inside of you, the blade is going inside of you. It's your ch—"

Ava brought her right foot up and slammed it down on his foot. When he stepped back in surprise, she brought her right hand up in an uppercut. The man's teeth clinked together and he reeled backwards. He swung out with the knife, but Ava blocked the blow easily. She captured his wrist and yanked up and backwards hard. The man screamed and tried slapping at her with his other hand. She leaned her head back, easily avoiding the desperate blows, and delivered two more quick jabs, one to the side of his head and the other to his nose. She saw his eyes roll back into his head and he collapsed to the ground. The knife clattered uselessly to the ground.

Confused and still wired on adrenaline, Ava looked from the man to the fence. She supposed this man had seen her coming, attracted by the commotion the hatchet-wielding man had caused. Drunk and armed, he'd apparently thought he'd be able to have his way with her. What he'd ended up getting instead was a broken nose and, whenever he came to, one hell of a headache. And maybe a fractured wrist.

She went over to the fence, realizing how badly her back and chest were aching from the failed assault of the fallen man behind her. She started making her way through the crack in the wooden fence only to realize that it was too late. She couldn't see the hatchet-wielding man, and the alley split into two directions, with a main street ahead. There was no telling where he had gone.

Massaging her right hand (that last jab she'd thrown had been a doozy, a rocket she'd learned to deliver while sparring at her father's gym), she quickly made her way back to the spot where she and Frances had come upon the fallen woman. Frances was blowing her whistle, the sound impossibly loud in the alley.

Ava looked down at the woman and cringed. Her legs stopped moving when she saw what had happened. Her stomach lurched a bit but she managed to get control of it.

There were two deep grooves etched into the woman's head—the same size as the blade of the hatchet the man had been carrying. One was chiseled into her head, tearing through her hair. The other was a bit lower, creasing across her brow. This one was obviously deeper, the blood pumping out in measures that made even the worst boxing matches Ava had ever seen look like nothing more than little paper cuts. But somehow, the worst part was the way the woman's eyes remained open, staring helplessly toward Ava.

She wasn't yet dead, but it wouldn't be long now. Frances was weeping softly as she continued to blow on her whistle. She did not look at Ava, likely angry that her partner had once again gone running off to play the hero.

Ava could not take her eyes off of the woman's gaze. She sank down, her chest still aching, and took the woman's hand. The woman gave Ava's hand a faint squeeze and her eyes grew hazy as Frances continued to blow on her whistle behind her. As for Ava, she couldn't find enough breath to blow into hers. All she could do was kneel there as the woman faded away, the already soft grip on Ava's hand eventually loosening completely.

CHAPTER SIX

Ava stood by quietly as the first two policemen arrived. By then, Frances's face was red and she looked to be on the verge of blacking out from blowing on her whistle so hard. The cops were an interesting pair: one was an older gentleman who seemed to almost be offended by the sight of the dead woman and the other was a younger chap who didn't seem bothered at all.

"How long have you been here?" the older cop asked.

"About five minutes," Ava said.

"And did you see the man that attacked her?" the younger asked, almost one question right behind the other.

"Yes," Ava said.

"Get a good look at him?"

Ava took a moment to consider her answer, but also knew it would only make matters worse if she lied about it. "I did," she said. "I chased after him for a moment, but all I ever really saw was his back."

"Was he a black man?" the cop asked.

"No. He was white." She hated that race was the first thing considered, but given this part of town, she supposed it made sense that was the first place he'd go. It still made her angry, though.

The policeman looked to Frances and said, "You're Mrs. Knight, correct?"

"I am."

Even standing in front of the dead body, Ava noticed that the policeman called Frances by the identifier of *Mrs.* rather than *Officer.*

"And you?" the policeman asked.

"Ava Gold. I'm…new."

"Clarence Gold's wife," the cop said thoughtfully as he slowly leaned down to look at the body. "You see the weapon he used?"

"Yes," Ava answered. "A hatchet. Almost like a meat cleaver."

"And you chased him, you say? In which direction?"

"Up this alley and then down two others. He escaped me when I was attacked."

"Attacked? The killer attacked you, too?"

"No, sir," she said. "It was someone else, someone—"

She was interrupted by the presence of another cop. This one was younger, but carried the look of authority well. The first two cops filled him in and within twenty seconds, it was almost as if Ava and Frances weren't even there. Just like that, it was a boys' club. When it was clear that any involvement in the case was about to be stripped from her, Ava decided it was time to speak up.

"I can give you a basic idea of where the killer escaped to," she said.

The older cop narrowed his eyes at her and gave her an *Oh, ain't that cute* sort of look.

"That won't be necessary," he said. "We'll take it from here." Then, as if considering some great problem, he added, "I don't suppose either of you know this lady?"

"No," Frances said.

"Stick around for a bit, would you?" the second cop on the scene said. "We'll need to get your full report on this."

Ava nodded, noticing that Frances had a defeated look on her face. Ava understood it, only she was pretty sure it was upsetting her more than Frances. They'd found the body, Ava had chased the killer down, and now their final contribution was going to be retelling the story so a bunch of men unfamiliar with the original scene could take over. In Ava's estimation, there was a fine line between being sexist and being dumb and ineffective—and these men were taking huge strides over that line.

Again, she felt the need to speak up. She wondered if she would have been able to stay quiet if the adrenaline from the chase and her own attack weren't still rushing through her. Add to that her ample dismantling of the man who tried to rape her and there was simply no way she could hold her tongue.

"I want to help," she said.

"Like I said," the second cop said, "you can give us your report in a moment and—"

"Let me on the case."

She saw Frances's eyes grow wide, replaced quickly with a frown. Apparently, as far as Frances was concerned, Ava was in the process of writing her own walking papers. However, there was a moment of amazement when the three cops shared a look, as if trying to communicate with only their minds. The elder cop looked from the body, then back to the women detectives. Any hope Ava had that they might be treated as equals was demolished when two of the three cops smiled at them.

The younger one shook his head and Ava found herself wanting to send a hard right-handed jab into his kisser.

"No, ladies," he said, clearly trying to hold in a giggle—even in the presence of this dead woman. "Your report will be enough."

Ava could only stand there as the case was stripped away from her. And as far as she was concerned, it was like swallowing acid.

***

Her father was sitting at the dinner table alone when she entered her apartment. She could see where he'd tried his best to throw dinner together—a slightly charred chicken and too-thick gravy.

"Long day, I take it?" Roosevelt asked.

"Yeah, that's for sure." She sat down at the table, feeling guilty and sad. No sign of Jeffrey meant he was probably already in bed. She knew she was late, but she didn't realize just how late until she'd entered the apartment. "Thanks, Dad."

"I'm happy to do it. I'm not happy that you weren't home when you said you'd be. You were supposed to pick Jeffrey up from the gym over two hours ago. I thought…" He stopped here, took a breath, and then looked at her with as much sincerity as he could muster. "Two hours late…I was worried something had happened to you."

"I really am sorry, Dad. There was a murder. "

His eyes grew wide and he grimaced slightly. He considered this for a while and Ava could feel his worry in the silence of the moment. "A murder?"

"Yes. And I'm sure they'll put the screws on me about it tomorrow."

"Why's that?"

"Because I chased after him. The Women's Bureau isn't supposed to do things like that. We're only to blow on our whistles and have the men come do the work."

The trace of a smile on Roosevelt's face almost made the tension of the afternoon worth it. "You get any punches in?"

She thought of the man who had tried assaulting her, and it wasn't a story she wanted to tell him. "One or two," she said, and left it at that.

Roosevelt nodded and pushed the remnants of the chicken toward her. "It's not great, but Jeffrey seemed to enjoy it. I let him help me cook it."

"How long has he been in bed?"

"Thirty minutes or so. I'm sure he's probably still up, waiting to say goodnight."

She tore a piece of meat from a chicken thigh and popped it into her mouth. It was dry and flavorless, but she was so hungry she barely noticed.

"Can I say something that may seem invasive?" Roosevelt said before she made her way to Jeffrey's room.

"Of course you can."

"I know Clarence would be proud of you for what you're doing. He'd be smiling and bragging his ass off to all of his buddies. But I also know that he wouldn't *expect it* of you. He'd be more worried about you raising Jeffrey into a respectable man. You don't need to pick up where he left off."

"I know. But I want to. I have to at least carry out his legacy. He was my hero, you know…right up there with Isabella Goodwin."

"The first female detective in New York, right?"

"Right. But the thing is, he wasn't only my hero. He was Jeffrey's hero, too. And this…this journey into the police department…is all about the man who killed him. He's still out there somewhere. And as a part of the Women's Bureau, I know my chances of being involved in his killer's capture is so incredibly small—but at least I'd be part of it."

She could tell that Roosevelt wanted to say something else. In the end, though, he simply got to his feet and came to her. He hugged her loosely (Roosevelt Burr had never been one for hugs) and whispered: "Just be careful. He's lost a father…it would ruin him if he lost you, too."

She turned away before the tears could start and walked down the small hallway to kiss her son goodnight. And even in that moment of sweetness, the statement she'd just spoken out loud rang in her ears. It seemed to circle her heart and land there, permanently becoming a part of her.

This journey into the police department is all about the man who killed him. He's still out there somewhere.

It was all the motivation she needed to continue trying to be Jeffrey's hero since his original hero had been so cruelly taken from him. And it gave her the motivation she needed, too. It helped her to decide that tomorrow morning, when she arrived at work, she was going to head straight to Minard's office and demand that he put her on the case.

CHAPTER SEVEN

The voice came back gradually, after having disappeared for about seven months. When it returned, he was not at all surprised to find that it was the voice of his mother. It made sense, he supposed. When he'd been discharged from the mental hospital, he'd gone back to the house he'd shared with his mother for all those years. And there in the corner was the chair she'd been sitting in when he'd killed her. Of course, no one knew *he* had killed her. Somehow, that connection had never been made. He guessed it was because he looked so innocent. He knew he looked borderline daft; he'd always had the look of a rube, a guy who might be just a little slow—the sort of fella his mother often said "looked a ham sandwich shy of a full picnic."

He heard her speaking up now, yelling in the hallways of his head. She usually quieted down when he left the house and wandered out onto the streets. The fresh air and the thick lanes of people moving along the sidewalks drowned her out. But it was almost as if she knew what he was up to today. It was like she knew where he was going and what he had planned.

You're sick, you know, she said. *All those treatments in the nuthouse did nothing, huh? Maybe they should have shocked you real good like they used to back in my day.*

A sick grin crept cross his face at the thought of his mother getting electric shocks. When he had been admitted to the mental institution, he'd been relieved to hear that such violent and barbaric treatments had been discontinued. Instead, they'd pumped him full of barbiturates and used a form of shock therapy that was much milder than what he'd been expecting.

The worst of it, though, had been the restraints. He'd pissed himself a few times because he had to use the bathroom during his episodes and no one would free him. When someone did finally come to him when his episode had passed, it was one of the nurses. He'd resented her for it and dreamed about killing her. She was a smart woman, much smarter than him, and making money with an honest job. Oh, the things she must have thought about him when she smelled his urine and had to change his sheets…

He had, of course, never gotten the chance to kill that nurse. In fact, it was shortly after he truly started to think about it that his head shrinker had deemed him fit to be discharged. And just like that, about five months after he'd been admitted into the psychiatric hospital, he was back on the same streets he'd been discovered in. He was still very hazy on how he'd even ended up there. He could recall being on the street, lost in the sounds of the women's political march, and then waking up with a headache as a cop looked down at him.

None of that mattered now, though. Now, he could only think of acting out. He had not killed the nurse, so his hands and heart ached for the death of something else. He wished it could be his nagging mother again, but regrettably, she was already gone. And there had been the woman yesterday, in the alley behind those deplorable jazz clubs, but that had barely scratched the itch.

He'd been walking the streets aimlessly for about a day or so. Some parts of it were little more than a blur, while others were crystal clear. He remembered wandering by jazz clubs and nightclubs just as dusk had fallen. He could recall a feeling of absolute sorrow in that he had been dealt a life that would not afford him such luxuries.

And that's when he spotted her. A woman, slightly taller than him, and probably about five years older. She was an absolute tomato, but she seemed to know it. She was much prettier than the woman in the alley yesterday. Even the way she clung to the arm of her fella screamed it. She was in charge…not linking arms with the man because she wanted it to be known that they were together, but because she was leading him along like a puppy on a leash. Her dress was white, a slit along the leg going all the way up past her knee. He thought of the treasures hidden slightly north of that slit in the dress and he'd become both aroused and enraged.

She was headed into one of the respectable clubs—the ballroom sort rather than the ones hidden in musty cellars to allow liquor and spirits to be passed about. Prohibition had really done a number on how the folks of New York partied after hours. Honestly, he thought it was all very stupid.

He walked back and forth along the block the nightclub was located on. He pretended to window-shop in front of a jewelry store. He went inside a candy shop and got a dime's worth of lemon drops. After grabbing a discarded newspaper, he pretended to read it on a bench just within view of the club. It was almost time for it to open, night having fallen and the crowd around the entrance getting thicker.

He saw her bob and weave in the crowd, laughing, clutching her gloved hand to her ample breast. Her black hair bobbing, her eyes cutting into everyone she saw as if she had already estimated them and knew he was so much better.

As the fine, spoiled people began to enter the club, he began to wonder how he might slip inside. He could get a second-rate suit, but he knew the folks inside the club would automatically look down on him.

It's because you're a joke, his mother spoke up in his head. *You're nothing but a failure, and that's all you'll ever be.*

"I put you in the damn ground, now didn't I?" he said from behind his newsprint.

He smiled as he recalled killing her—the way the blood sprayed, the way her eyes were so shocked that he'd had it in him in her last living moments, Only, when he replayed it in his head, it was not his mother's face he saw but that of the elegant, confident woman he'd spied earlier—the woman who had just entered the club. He saw her pretty eyes, wide and pleading, and it sparked a restlessness within him that he knew could not be stopped until she was dead.

CHAPTER EIGHT

Ava walked Jeffrey to school the following morning, a nice walk of about four blocks—and, she supposed, a good way to warm up for walking her patrol. And while she enjoyed the time with her son, her mind was also on what she was going to do when she got to the precinct. She had already decided she was going to go straight to Minard but she had not decided how to handle the rejection she'd surely get. He would tell her no; she was sure of that. He'd tell her no if for no other reason than to discourage her and get her to quit.

She shook those thoughts away as she stopped half a block shy, giving Jeffrey the little bit of freedom he'd asked for when it came to school. She stood under the awning of a butcher shop and watched him walk through the gates. He was talking with friends within a few seconds, heading into the school building. She was a little uneasy with him walking from school to the boxing club later on, but Jeffrey was a smart kid. He knew the areas to stay away from and had a good head on him. She figured she had to start trusting him completely at some point—especially now that there wasn't a father figure to help teach him the ropes. Deep down, she wondered if that was one of the reasons she'd wanted a job at the precinct—to fill the shoes that Jeffrey needed to be filled whether he knew it or not.

It had started spitting rain by the time she got to the precinct—not even a drizzle, really, just enough to dampen things a bit. As she walked toward the doors, images from yesterday's murder scene popped up in her head. She saw the gouges in the woman's head so clearly that it was almost as if she were lying right there in front of the precinct door. She shook it off, knowing that the case would be well on its way to being solved by the time she started today's patrol. Even if her only contribution was the discovery of the body, that would be enough. It would *have* to be.

She headed straight to Captain Minard's office, walking sternly, as if she was not nervous at all. When she reached his office at the end of the primary hallway, she found the door closed. She knocked, but got no answer. She figured he hadn't gotten into the office yet or was already out on police business. She stared at the door for a moment, determined not to let this little setback change her mind about confronting him.

It felt like defeat, though, and she wasn't quite ready to venture into the WB office in such a mood. She decided she'd go to the rather small women's locker room to fix up her hair, maybe wash the smell of dish soap from the morning's chores from her hand. She did not mind the job of being mother at all, but she did not see the point in bringing the scents and cornerstones of it to work. It had been a good morning. She'd played jazz, starting with Jelly Roll Morton but switching it to something more acceptable, like Louis Armstrong, when Jeffrey had come into the kitchen, complaining. She'd told him a bit about her days as a singer over a breakfast of eggs and toast and for a moment, she'd gotten a good feel for what life was going to be like without Clarence. It was going to be very hard, but she thought they'd be okay.

She went to the little downstairs locker room and washed her hands with the very strong lye soap on the sink. As she looked herself over in the mirror, she saw two things: one, that her hair looked just fine, though a bit damp from the misting rain outside; second, there were two men standing back in the entrance to the locker room. Having been spotted, the first one grinned at her and came forward. When he did, she saw that there were actually three of them. They were all wearing police uniforms but this did very little to ease her mind. The looks on their faces were filled with spite and some sort of sport—particularly the one in front.

"Fitting in well here?" the guy in front said. He was a younger guy, maybe Ava's own age. Behind him, she recognized one of the faces. The man in back had showed up at the murder scene yesterday.

"As well as can be expected," Ava answered honestly.

"Good," the lead cop said. He kept walking forward, making no sign of slowing. Ava backed up a bit until her lower back connected with the sink. The man came closer still, no less than six inches between them now.

"You know, Clarence spoke highly of you," he said. "Always going on and on about his pretty wife. And now that you're here…damn if he wasn't right."

He reached out and placed his hand on her hip. He pulled her closer and brought his hand up higher, just below her breast. "One of these days, I may just have to find out what you're like outside of work," he said.

One of the men behind him chuckled. Ava was growing scared, but she wasn't sure how scared to be. How far would these men take this?

She decided she had no interest in finding out. As the man in front of her leaned even closer, pressing his chest against her, Ava drew her right hand back and delivered a hard jab to the man's ribs. He doubled over and when he did, she tossed out another jab that clipped his jaw. He went falling backward, but that wasn't good enough for Ava.

As he staggered, she came around with a surprise left that caught him in the face. It was the sort of punch that would leave a blackened eye and a hell of a lot of swelling. The cop went to the floor in a heap, but Ava did not give herself time to enjoy the sight. She looked instantly to the other two, fully expecting them to come charging at her.

They did nothing of the sort, though. In fact, the one in the back turned away instantly and made his exit. The other one looked at the fallen cop with something very close to awe on his face. When he did look back at Ava, there was no malice on his face. *My God,* Ava thought. *Is that respect I see?*

She stepped away from the sinks, around the fallen cop, and to the door. The third cop did not move, and he said nothing. Flexing her wrist a bit from the slight pain of that last punch, Ava left the locker room. She knew the instance would not be reported. There was no way a male cop—especially a young one with everything to prove—would admit that a dame had cooled him so easily.

She felt taken advantage of and slightly embarrassed but she also could not deny the little spark of pleasure that bounced around within her as she made her way to the WB office, ready for her third day on the job.

She barely had time to sit down at her desk before Frances was calling over to her. "You ready to head out, Gold?"

"Already?"

Frances nodded, frowning. "He's trying hard to get under your skin, it seems."

Ava thought of that closed door, wondering if Minard had been in there all along but simply had no interest in anything she had to say.

Well, screw him, she thought. *He's not going to win this easily.*

"Sure. Let's head out."

As she and Frances made their way out of the office, she noticed the looks some of the other WB officers were giving her. Some, like Lottie, gave her encouraging glances, obviously rooting for her. Others frowned and barely met her gaze, as if they were certain she'd eventually break under the pressure.

When they were out of the office and heading up the stairs to the main floor Frances looked at her and asked, "Are you okay, Gold?"

"Yeah. Why?"

"You look upset about something. Sort of…I don't know…*stern.*"

It killed her not to tell Frances about the altercation in the locker room. She figured telling *anyone* would draw attention to it and there would be a chance that rumors and gossip would get to the higher-ups such as Captain Minard. So as far as Ava was concerned, it would be an event that would never be spoken about…and she thought that might be to her benefit.

"No, I'm good."

Frances let it rest at that as they made their way out onto the streets. It continued to rain softly as they were out on their patrol. They both carried department-issued umbrellas, but they opted not to use them. The slight pattering of rain simply didn't warrant it.

Now on her third patrol, Ava started to notice a few things. First of all, there was no need for her and Frances to fill the silence with talking. Whenever Ava had a question—for instance, what the hard and fast rules were on loitering—Frances was happy to answer it. But other than a few instances of this, they walked their patrol mostly in silence.

It allowed Ava to get a better feel for her city—for how it continued to grow and expand. She could swear there was a heartbeat to the place beneath the bustling businesses, the streets that still catered to horse-drawn carriages but were already evolving to adapt to the Model Ts and other scant automobiles. It was certainly a growing city, a city she felt would never stop shifting and changing. Clarence had often told her he sometimes felt like New York City was a living, breathing thing that would never be fed enough. He'd even said something in that regard on their first date, after he'd seen her singing at one of the jazz clubs just outside of Harlem.

She was pulled out of her thoughts of Clarence as male voice called out, high and shrill. "Come on over here, sweetie! I'll let you arrest me. Maybe even let you slap those handcuffs on me!"

She looked over to a construction site and saw two men standing on scaffolding, looking down at her. Her face flushed with anger but she kept her comments to herself. It wasn't like it was the first time she'd been hollered at by a jobbie during her three patrols.

"Charming, huh?" Frances said. "I never understood it…the way men just holler stuff like that at ladies. They expecting to get lucky with comments like that? Ask Lottie all about that when you get the chance. Not too long ago, a man yelled at her that he wanted to eat lunch off of her backside. When she told him she'd consider it if he did the cooking, I thought the guy was going to fall right off his ladder."

Ava heard her, but the smile on her face was only obligatory. She realized, having been so rudely pulled out of her thoughts, that they were now only two blocks away from the alley where they'd discovered the woman yesterday. She heard the light thrum of a bass from a soundcheck somewhere ahead, but even that was muted.

It was even harder because she had once sung as a back-up singer at the club next door. It was a small place, smoky and a little questionable, to be honest. Somehow, the murder seemed to have struck her as a personal attack because of this. She realized just how selfish this was, which was why she'd said nothing to Frances about it yesterday—the reason, in fact, she had done her very best to push the thought all the way back to the furthest cobwebbed corners of her mind.

"Yeah, it can give you the willies," Frances said.

"What's that?"

"Returning to the scene of a crime so soon. Especially one like yesterday. You need to go a few blocks over?"

"No, I'm good."

Frances hesitated a moment and then decided she was apparently telling the truth. They walked on a few more blocks and passed by the alley. Ava barely looked down it, somehow certain another body would be there. And beyond that body, another man lurking in the shadows, anxious to assault any woman dumb enough to go traipsing around in the shadows.

But even then, the club just ahead grabbed her concentration. She'd managed to avoid looking at it yesterday, not wanting to mar her fond memories of the place. It truly was a little hole-in-the-wall dive, a small club overshadowed by some of the larger ones. But the crowds had always been appreciative of the talent and even after prohibition had made it harder to get booze. Moods had always been lively. Called the Key Factory, it was where Ava truly got her start in singing for jazz bands—where she'd truly started to entertain her dream of one day being a jazz singer.

"You know," she said, on the verge of telling Frances about that certain part of her history. But before she got it out, she saw something rather odd.

Ahead of them, a detective walked into the Key Factory. He did so quickly, as if not wanting to be seen by anyone. If he noticed Ava and Frances, he made no indication.

"I know what?" Frances asked.

"Nothing. Did you see that? The detective that just went in that club?"

"Yeah. And good for him. He's likely been assigned to the case from yesterday."

"Likely…" Ava said.

Before she knew it, her legs were carrying her in that direction. Frances followed, confused. "What are you doing?"

"I want to go inside. I know this place."

"No, Ava. You can't interfere in the case."

"It's not interfering if I'm helping, right?"

"I wish. Look, I know it seems unjust, but we're women. We can't just—"

But Ava was already reaching for the door. As she opened it, a wave of familiarity washed over her, drowning out Frances's curses and objections from behind.

CHAPTER NINE

The familiarity of the place rocked her harder than she expected. She was dizzy for a moment, realizing that this place, in a small way, had once been a part of her life.

Frances wasted no time in voicing her displeasure. "Gold, you need to come back out on the street with me," Frances said. "Being here is going to do nothing but get us in trouble. And you're okay in my book, but I'm not going to lose my job for you."

"Then go back outside," Ava said, not realizing how rude it sounded until it was out of her mouth. "This place feels almost like home to me. I feel…*safe* here."

Ava allowed herself a moment to appreciate the familiarity of the Key Factory. It had been nearly two years since she last stepped foot in here, to sing on the stage with some very talented up-and-coming jazz musicians. Even now, before the night crowd seeped in, the place smelled of cigarette and reefer smoke, of sweat and cheap cologne and perfume. In the presence of it all, it was hard to remember why she'd stopped singing. The bare board floors, the little tables that looked like they might fall apart at any moment, the harsh overhead lights…it was all calling her back. But life had evolved: Jeffrey had gotten older and needed help with school, and Clarence's work schedule was hectic and unpredictable. It had just not worked out for a singer who needed to be in places like this past midnight.

She shook the impending sense of regret away when she spotted the detective over at one of the tables near the center of the room. She recognized the man he was speaking to. He was a co-owner of the Key Factory, a gaunt-looking bruno named Jack Dooley. He wore eyeglasses that made him look refined, and he kept his moustache neat and tidy. But it was all just a ruse, as he was one of the crudest businessmen Ava had ever met. But he knew good music and had never had a cross word with Ava or any of her supporting musicians.

She could tell from the look on his face that Jack was irritated. She'd seen that look many times as he'd spoken to difficult musicians and rowdy patrons. She also knew that Jack was not the sort of man to crack. The look on his face did make her wonder what, exactly, the detective was asking. Ever the opportunist, Ava walked toward the table. She hesitated, sensing the importance of the moment, but pushed herself on regardless. She faintly heard Frances hissing her name behind her.

As Ava approached the table, she started to hear some of what Jack was saying. And yes, he *was* irritated. She knew that Jack and his co-owner ran a basement speakeasy out of the Key Factory so even if he *wanted* to be cooperative (which was unlikely), he would keep his trap shut.

"…and you coppers are always just looking for reasons to snoop around our clubs," Jack was saying. "I wasn't born yesterday. Sorry, mac, but unless you have a warrant or an actual reason to be in here snooping around, I need you to leave."

The detective—a handsome forty-something gentleman with salt and pepper hair and a thick jaw—grimaced. He looked like a cool, refined sort…but also the sort of man who would lose that very same cool over something small and insignificant. Ava could see it in the way he furrowed his brow, as if he were resting all of his burdens there, waiting at any moment for it to all slide off and crack open his frustrations. The irritation in his expression was obvious. Ava could see that he was about to get up from the table.

"Now, Jack," Ava said, putting far more cheer into her voice than she was accustomed to. "Is that any way to speak to a guest?"

Jack Dooley looked up at her, genuinely confused for a moment. But when the recognition landed, his face lit up and he sprang up out of his chair. "Hot damn! Ava Gold, where the hell have you been?"

He lumbered over and gave her an immense hug. The detective watched this all with mild annoyance; Ava caught a peek of his expression from over Jack's shoulder. Jack broke the hug, looked at her with great interest for a moment, and then frowned.

"Ava, my lovely, I'd love to chin with you a bit, but as you can see, I'm having to entertain the fuzz today."

"Now, Mr. Dooley," the detective said, "you aren't trying to get lippy with me, are you?" He then cut his eyes toward Ava and said, "And Ava Gold, don't you think I don't know who you are. You have no business here and I think I can handle this on my own."

"Hey, now," Jack said angrily. "Mrs. Gold is a dear friend of mine and I won't—"

Ava cut him off with the wave of a hand. She glanced back and saw Frances watching the scene play out. She looked absolutely mortified.

"He's right, Jack. It might upset you to know that I'm a copper now." She gave him a playful smile and then, under her breath, said, "But they sure as hell don't treat me like a cop."

"You pulling my leg?"

"Not at all. I'm brand new, a member of the Women's Bureau." She showed him the whistle around her neck and said, "Why else would I carry around this ridiculous thing?"

"Well then, *Officer* Gold," Jack said. "Why don't you take some notes from this here Detective Wimbly on how to *not* go about asking people for information?"

"Hold it right there," Wimbly said, getting to his feet. "How do you two know one another?"

"Once upon a time," Jack said, "Ava Gold was one of the better jazz singers to grace the stage at the Key Factory. At a few other places in town I won't name, too. If she really is working for your kind, I consider it a miserable waste of talent."

"I appreciate that," Ava said. "But listen, Jack: there was a woman killed out in that alley back behind your club yesterday. I'm pretty sure Detective Wimbly is just trying to get to the bottom of it."

"Oh, I'm sure of that," Jack said. "But he's going about it as if he owns my club. And you know how it is in establishments like this. The cops are always looking for some excuse to push in on you, to bully in and get whatever they want. Come in just to check a so-called suspect and end up closing the damned place down."

"Mr. Dooley, I'm not—" Wimbly started.

But Ava interrupted him. Wimbly looked as if someone had socked him right in the jaw. She heard Frances shifting uncomfortably behind her.

"Now, Jack, do you think I'd be vouching for someone who would do that to you?"

Jack sighed and looked back and forth between them—which was rather awkward, as Ava had never met Wimbly before. Right now, she was trying not only to reconnect with an old friend, but to prove a point to Wimbly and the rest of the male police force. For all she knew, Wimbly could be just as bad as the jabroni she'd decked in the locker room this morning. But in the moment, this felt right.

"What do you need to know, Ava?" Jack asked. He gave Wimbly what Clarence had always called a pie-eating grin when he asked her directly.

"You knew there had been a murder, right?" Ava asked.

"I did. A bad one, too."

Wimbly spoke up, making sure not to be omitted. "Her name was Evelyn White. Did you know her?"

When Jack answered, he was still looking only at Ava. "Not well, but yes, I knew who she was. She came in here from time to time for some early sets. A looker, that's for sure. But she was rarely here with the same man twice. That sort of lady, you know?"

"Did she ever cause trouble?" Ava asked. "Maybe flirt a little too much and get two fellas squawking over her?"

"No, nothing like that."

"Can you remember anything at all about her? Anything that sticks out?"

"She was really big into the women's movement," Jack said. "She was in here sometimes with a lot of other ladies making all kinds of fuss about politics and voting and all that. Nothing bad but, you know…she wanted to be noticed."

"Can you think of any men she might have been with who were men of influence?" Ava asked.

Jack thought about it for a moment and shook his head. "Nope, Just a bunch of average Joes as far as I can tell."

Ava looked over to Detective Wimbly and shrugged. "Anything you'd like to add, Detective?"

Wimbly looked dumbfounded at first but then nodded. "Shoot straight with me, Mr. Dooley. Are there normally any criminal activities conducted in that alley?"

The bit of clam Jack had managed to claim dissolved slowly. "You know, there are at least three other businesses on this street that share that alley! Have you questioned them as thoroughly? But to answer your question, the only crimes I know of that take place in that alley from time to time are sex crimes…but all consensual, if you get my drift."

Ava watched Wimbly struggle to find a response or another question, but there was nothing.

"Now, can I get back to work?"

Wimbly seemed hesitant to answer, so Ava did it for him. "Yes, Jack. Thanks for your help. And it sure is good seeing you again."

"You need to get yourself back up on my stage," Jack said.

"Maybe one day." Though deep down, she honestly didn't know if it was true. She hadn't given it any honest thought for several months. And now with Clarence gone, it seemed like a very distant dream.

As Jack made his way to the other side of the club, back behind the little food counter where drinks used to be served, Ava looked at

Wimbly. She figured she deserved the verbal lashing she was about to get. She knew she'd stepped way out of line just to prove a point and now she was going to pay for it.

Instead, she got something a little different. Wimbly got to his feet and gave her a very faint smile. "I gotta tell you, Gold…you've gone and put me right behind the eight ball."

"How's that?"

"Well, your endless guts for one. I can't deny that you're either brave or really dumb. And I doubt Clarence Gold married himself a dumb broad. On top of that, you did a fine job of questioning him. Old acquaintance or not, it's plain to see you have a shine for this."

She had not been expecting the compliments—backhanded or not. She was taken aback for a second, but managed to keep some semblance of control.

"And that troubles you?" Ava asked. She was faintly aware that Frances had tiptoed forward to get an ear in.

"Me, personally? No. But I sort of get the sense you're going to cause some trouble along the way. If you make it, of course."

He gave her another smile and headed for the door. Frances approached her and gave her a stern look that was betrayed by the happiness in her eyes.

"One of these days, you're going to cause me to have a stroke," Frances said. "But honestly…if you can keep putting men in their place like that, it might very well be worth it."

"Let's not get too excited," Ava said as they walked back to the door, several paces behind Wimbly. "I might have gotten Jack Dooley to talk, but we still don't have any answers."

"Your use of the word *we* scares me," Frances said. "You know you can't just go off looking into this case as if you were a male police officer, right?"

Ava chose to say nothing, still lightly floating on the compliments Wimbly had given her. Yet as they headed back out onto the street, she was reminded of her vow to speak directly with Captain Minard, requesting that she be put on the case. She was going to get it done, and there was no amount of violent, self-involved men attacking her in locker rooms in the world that was going to stop her.

She was going to ask to be put on the case. She was going to be firm and direct with Minard—and if she was laughed out of the building, so be it. At least she had tried. At least she had not settled for the WB basement when she knew she had so much more to offer.

CHAPTER TEN

As casually as he could, he moved away from under the sundry store canopy. He pretended to check a watch he wasn't even wearing, and then started walking forward. He held his left arm close to him, securing the handle of the hatchet that was tucked into his pants. It made walking a bit difficult and every now and then the point along the end of the blade nicked him slightly. That was okay, though; he rather enjoyed it.

He studied her perfect curves and golden hair. As he did, the voice in his head was louder than ever. The shrill, phantomlike voice of his mother, teasing and taunting. Tonight, his latest object of interest had made a serious mistake; she had come out with friends. They were all pretty, though in a vain and almost glaring way. The way the men they passed all looked at them was clearly what they were going for. Just another way to lure…another way to control. They now had the right to vote, had a visible dream of equality, and some of them sure as hell had let it go to their head.

The night seemed to go his way near midnight when the three of them came out of the club. He was already a bit ahead of the direction he knew she would be walking—to her little apartment maybe. Or possibly her parents' place. He still wasn't sure if she was living alone or with her parents. Not that it mattered. She wouldn't be making it back there tonight—especially given that one of her friends had come out of the club clinging to a large man smoking a cigar. He watched as she drunkenly waved goodbye to her friends, her arm around the man's waist, his hand on her ass.

He had been following her for a few days now, so he knew where she lived. He also knew that she believed she was untouchable—that none of life's burdens and sadness would ever befall her. Perhaps that's why she thought her friend was enough protection as she walked the half a mile from the club to her home.

But he also knew where this friend lived. They'd chatted on her stoop from time to time. And it was there that he planned to make his move. He could see it up ahead right now, a well-to-do little apartment building. A lone man sat on the stoop, writing in a book and smoking a cigarette.

He hurried his pace just a bit, his head lowered and looking at the street. When he passed the friend's stoop, a flurry of excitement erupted in his heart. It took everything within him not to pull out the hatchet. He started nervously muttering to himself. He was aware of it, and he did his best to keep it quiet. He thought of his mother and the hatchet and it was all he could do to contain himself.

He heard her laughing softly somewhere behind him. When he came to the edge of the apartment building, he eyed the alley up ahead, between another apartment building and a tailor's shop.

Look at you, his mother's voice said. *Hiding in the shadows like a damn coward…*

He shut the voice down, willing a dark curtain to come down in his mind over it—over *everything* except the woman at the stoop.

Somewhere behind him, he heard the smoking man speak to them. "It's late at night for two beauties like you to be walking home alone, isn't it?"

He smiled; things just couldn't get any better. If questions arose later, the friend would certainly remember the smoking man with his journal and his comment.

As the women made muttered responses, he slipped into the alleyway. It was grimy and dark. No one else inhabited it, though he did see a stray dog lying sleepily against the tailor's shop a bit farther back.

He listened to them chatting, laughing. He feared his lady might go inside and enjoy herself a bit more, maybe a few more drinks if her friend had somehow managed to procure a bottle or two somewhere along the line. After all, prohibition in New York City was taken seriously, but it was quite easy to get your hands on some juice if you knew where to look.

But no…he heard them utter a few goodbyes. And then he heard her footsteps. The smoking man said nothing else, and he could imagine the bastard eyeing his lady from behind.

He pulled out the hatchet and waited. Time seemed to freeze and even his breath felt like it had stopped. He heard her coming and imagined he could even smell her—her perfume, her sweat, the liquor that was surely on her breath.

He took a deep breath and then there she was. He saw her hair fluttering in the breeze, almost golden, and then her shoulder. Reaching out with his free hand, he clutched her and pulled her into the alley.

She opened her mouth to scream, but he'd already brought the hatchet around. It landed just above her left eye and the impact of it caused the fingers gripping the hatchet to shudder. Her knees went out and she collapsed to the ground. He hunkered down, seeing that she was still breathing and trembling. He drew the hatchet back and buried it again.

In that moment, the sound it made was the only noise in the world.

It was even louder than his mother's voice in his head and for that, he was grateful.

<h1 style="text-align:center">CHAPTER ELEVEN</h1>

Ava was walking Jeffrey to school and her mind was so obsessed with thoughts of the case that she barely heard the two men in front of her. They were speaking visually, as well-to-do men often did on their way to work.

"You hear about this?" the well-dressed man in the fedora said to the man walking beside him. He held a newspaper out to his friend. "Seems there's madman loose."

"Yeah," the other man said, glancing at the newspaper. "It's a damn shame."

Ava, who had barely even looked at the newspaper, glanced ahead curiously to see what they were talking about. She wondered if it was another article about the murder of Evelyn White.

"I beg your pardon," Ava said, hurrying forward a bit. "A madman?"

Both men turned around. They were well-dressed and very clean—likely bankers or lawyers. There were quite a few of them on the streets around the area of Jeffrey's school in the mornings, on the way to work.

"So sorry," the man with the paper said. "Wasn't trying to spook the boy."

"No, it's not that. I just…I heard about that woman the other day."

"Oh, well, looks like there's been another. Last night, in fact." He showed her the paper, keeping it high up as if to protect Jeffrey's eyes from the headlines.

The story wasn't the main headline (she imagined the story was far too recent to snatch that amount of weight) but was on the front page, near the bottom. The headline read: *Second victim of 'hatchet-killer' found moments after death!*

"This happened last night?" she asked the men.

"It sure did. It's just not a safe city any more. It's getting too damned big." He frowned, looked at Jeffrey, and then offered the paper to Ava. "Help yourself, ma'am. And do keep safe."

Ava read the article, though there was not much. A woman named Annie Tate had been killed on her way home from a high-end club last night. She had been stabbed in the head with what appeared to be the same weapon that had killed Evelyn White. She was killed in an alley just a block away from her best friend's apartment and less than four blocks from her own home. The article ended stating the police seem ill prepared to handle an ever-growing population where many people think they can get away with pretty much anything.

"You okay, Mom?" Jeffrey asked.

"Yes," she said. "Just a very sad story. But you don't need to hear about that." She tucked the newspaper under her arm and took his hand.

"Is it about cop stuff?" he asked, undeterred.

"Yes, it is. But you don't need to worry about cop stuff. You need to worry about school stuff."

"Is it okay for me to tell everyone at school you're with the police now?" he asked. He looked to the ground when he asked, as if he was slightly embarrassed.

"That's your choice," she said. "I know you were very proud to tell everyone your dad was a police officer. You just need to know that some people don't think women really deserve a place with the police."

"Well, that's dumb."

"I'm glad you think so," she said as his school came into view. She knelt down and gave him a hug. "Take it easy on Grandpa this evening. I should be there to pick you up on time today."

Jeffrey hugged her back in a way growing kids did—fierce, but brief. She watched him hurry across the street, pausing for a puttering black Studebaker. When she turned her eyes back to the newspaper, it was quite a contrast. But it also got her hurrying to work, now more eager than ever to speak with Captain Minard about being put on this case. She could not quite figure out why, but she felt close to these crimes now—perhaps because she, like the witness in the story, had seen this killer and had been unable to stop him.

As she recalled that moment, the case felt more than just *close* to her. It felt personal.

***

She heard the commotion from within the precinct before she'd even opened the doors. Urgent voices and the sounds of many people in motion only amplified when she *did* open them. She found the place in chaos. Closest to her, there were two policemen yelling at a cowering man holding a pad and a pen. She assumed this was a reporter, perhaps coming by to get a statement on the hatchet killings. Not too far away from them, there were several people going through a filing cabinet in a hurry, tearing through records and files in search of something in particular. Along the right wall, she saw a receptionist running quickly with papers in her hand, headed to the back offices. Near the center of the primary bullpen just off the welcome desk, she saw Captain Minard speaking loudly to a group of about a dozen policemen. He was holding the morning paper in his hand.

Ava stepped forward slowly, realizing that by tuning in and out of every situation currently taking place, she was able to piece together bits of conversation that told her everything taking place. It wasn't much more information than she'd found in the article, but it was better than nothing, she supposed.

Annie Tate was a vocal women's rights advocate, a member of several organizations that encouraged women to get out and campaign for political candidates. The fact that Evelyn White had also been deeply involved and vocal about women's rights had been noted, linked, and was currently being looked into.

As she walked closer to where Minard was speaking loudly to the dozen policemen, she got more information. "The guys at the morgue are saying the wounds line up perfectly with those found on Evelyn White. It's certainly the same hatchet. As for the man who's doing it, all we have to go on is that he is of average height and weight. And apparently damned fast. And strong, if the depth of these hatchet strikes is any indication." He sighed and tossed the newspaper down on the ground, as if in disgust. "Boys, be careful out there. This isn't some overzealous drunk selling illegal booze. This man is a killer. And just because it seems he's chosen pretty young ladies as his targets, we can't assume he won't attack if provoked. So get out there and do your jobs…but do them safely and responsibly."

He gave a single, loud clap of the hands and the cops dispersed quickly. A few of them nudged past Ava on their way out, giving her untrusting glances. Deep down, she knew the timing was terrible, but Ava walked forward anyway. She was going to get a moment of Minard's time before he got swamped again. As she did, she could still hear the cops berating the reporter behind her. One of them was cursing him out, claiming that the bad press was unfair. She knew this was usually true, just based on some of the stories Clarence had told her. Sometimes if there was a particularly bad crime and the police hadn't figure it all out within a few hours, it was seen as incompetence. And even Ava knew that wasn't fair.

Minard had started moving away, back toward his office. Ava summed up her nerve and called out "Captain?"

He wheeled around with the impatience of a man who clearly did not want to be bothered. When he saw that it was Ava approaching he made no attempt to hide the disdain on his face.

"Mrs. Gold, as you can see, we're slightly busy here. A potential mass murderer running loose in the city tends to do that. So please…make sure what you want to tell me is important."

Ava was mortified to find that the words did not want to come out. They were right there on her tongue, but she could not quite get them out. When she finally did manage to speak them, they came out like stones from her mouth, the words heavy and seeming to fall from the floor.

"Let me help with this."

He looked at her like she'd just told him a joke that he didn't understand. "Get down to the WB, Gold."

"Sir, I saw this guy. I chased him. I can—"

"Yes, you chased him. You chased him and he got away."

She bit back a barbed retort and instead opted for: "But my description of him can—"

"Your description of him has been taken down by police much more experienced and capable than you. Now…this is your last warning. Get yourself down to the WB. If you want to help, then do the job you asked for."

He turned so quickly that even if Ava could have thought of a fitting response, she would not have had time to give it. With fury and disappointment mingling like a poisonous cocktail in her stomach, Ava marched toward the stairs to the WB. On the way, she passed by a familiar face—Detective Wimbly, watching her closely from his desk in the bullpen.

This somehow only infuriated her further. She fought tears of anger away as she made her way through the busy precinct, thinking that, Nineteenth Amendment or not, some things in this messed up world would never truly change.

But maybe she would be the exception. Before long, she'd know the answer because she sure as hell didn't intend to stop.

CHAPTER TWELVE

Detective Frank Wimbly had watched the entire exchange. He watched as Ava Gold boldly made her way over to Captain Minard, and then cringed a bit when he saw how Minard responded. He spoke down to her as if she were a stubborn child, making absolutely no attempt to even pretend that what she had to say mattered. Frank had the utmost respect for Captain Minard, but he thought the interaction with Ava was shameful—especially after all that her husband had given to this police force.

As the chaos continued around him, Frank rubbed his hands together nervously (something he did when he was in deep thought) and watched Minard weave his way back to his office.

"What are you doing, Wimbly?" Frank asked himself, a little surprised at himself.

He got to his feet and headed in the same direction. He knew Minard liked him and maybe even respected him over most of the other coppers. Frank had been around a while and, as a detective, had a sort of intangible edge that the other buttons in the precinct simply didn't have. Minard seemed to know this and value it. Frank just hoped it paid off in the next several minutes.

He watched Minard enter his office, closing the door behind him. Undaunted, Frank continued forward. He was at the closed door ten seconds later. He hesitated for a moment, wondering if this was only going to add fire to an already sizzling powder keg. Throwing caution to the wind, he raised his hand and knocked.

"What?" was the response from the other side of the door. Not a good sign at all.

"It's Frank, sir," he called through the door "Permission to enter?"

"Yeah, Frank, come on in." There was no irritation or hesitation in his voice. Maybe it wouldn't be so bad after all.

Frank stepped inside the captain's office. It was cluttered with three chairs, two filing cabinets, and a large desk stacked with files and assorted papers. A newer model typewriter sat on the far edge, a sheet of paper rolled in.

"Please tell me you have an insight into this hatchet killer," Minard said, sighing and reclining back in his chair.

"I think you're doing all you can right now. I think it's just a matter of asking the right people the right questions. But if I may…?"

Minard gave him a simple nod. His eyes were inquisitive now, perhaps hoping for some helpful information or guidance.

"I saw Ava Gold approach you a minute or so ago. And forgive me for saying so, sir, but I think you're missing a golden opportunity…as it were."

"She's too new," Minard said. "And a woman! You noticed that, correct?"

"Yes, sir, I'm aware."

"Clarence Gold was a hell of an officer, but—"

"And his loss is fresh on everyone's minds," Wimbly said. "Not only that, but yesterday when I was out over in Harlem trying to get some details about Evelyn White, she showed up with Frances Knight. She was able to draw information out of a potential lead who would have nothing to do with me. Now, it was because they had a history, but the way she did it…sir, she knows what she's doing."

"I appreciate your concern, Frank. But if I let even one broad from the Women's Bureau get involved in a case like this, I'd be laughed out of town."

"Unless she succeeds. Unless she just happens to be the widow of one of the best officers we ever had. All of that commotion outside…it's because we know the city is going to get scared. But if we allow Ava Gold to actively take part in the investigation, it will distract from that. Hell, to the female population that has a right to be scared of this killer, it may even bring them some hope. Sir…a woman on the case could look *good* for us…for *you*."

Minard hung his head, shaking it slowly. "The absolute shit of it is that you're absolutely right. But she…" He stopped here and sighed. "Yesterday with this lead, was she professional?"

"Mostly. She went the personal route. Trying to appeal to them, trying to relate."

Giving an even heavier sigh, Minard picked the receiver up from the wall-mounted phone behind him. He dialed three numbers, the insides of the telephone whirring and chugging along.

"You'll keep an eye on her?" Minard said.

"If that's what it ta—"

But he was interrupted as Minard spoke to the other end of the line.

"Mrs. Knight, it's Captain Minard. Send Ava Gold up to my office, would you?"

When she stepped into the office and saw not only Minard, but Detective Wimbly as well, Ava was certain that she was in trouble. Had she overstepped yesterday? Had Wimbly seriously come complaining to Minard and now, with the final tipping point of approaching the captain earlier this morning, she was going to be released from her position? Did he understand just how badly she needed this job? Did he understand she had a boy to raise, an apartment to pay for?

She didn't want to close the door behind her but felt it was the expected thing to do. When it was closed, she was not asked to sit down. Instead, Minard stared her down hard. Wimbly looked expectantly at Minard, waiting for something.

"Mrs. Gold, level with me," Minard said. "You asked for this job at Clarence's wake. I'm no fool. I know you have goals of some sort of vengeance for his death by working here, hoping to catch bad people, is that right?"

"Yes." She did not see the point in denying it.

"If I put you on this hatchet killer case, will you be able to take that need for vengeance and place it far away in the back of your mind? Police work is not about vengeance. It's about keeping others safe and upholding the law. Motivation is fine. Revenge is often a great motivator. But it can't be your *goal*. Do you understand?"

She was still hung up on the first part of the statement, the part where he'd said *If I put you on this case.* But she understood the totality of it, so she nodded and said, "Yes, sir."

"Detective Wimbly said you showed some interrogative skill when you ran into him yesterday, and I trust him. But I don't trust a woman with a vendetta."

"I understand."

"Now, for the sake of being honest with you—this is also about spinning a story. A woman cop on the hunt for a woman-killer in a city that is still, even ten years later, celebrating women's voting rights being passed. So if you're on this case, you're a cop first. You *will* remain professional. Any bad press you cause will not knock you back down to the WB office—it will be the end of your job here."

Ava could only nod. She did her best not to seem shocked. She was getting what she had asked for, but was now hearing the cost of it. "When...when do I start?"

"Right now. You'll be partnered with Detective Wimbly on an unofficial basis."

Apparently, this was news to Wimbly; he flinched and gave Minard a confused look. When Minard was clearly not going to say anything on the matter, Wimbly straightened out his face.

"That's it," Minard said. "Get to work."

Ava turned and opened the door. When she stepped back out into the precinct, she let out a huge breath, not realizing until then that she had been holding it in while in the office. Triumph flared within her, but it was brief.

Holy God, she thought. *Somehow…somehow I'm a detective. Clarence, keep an eye out for me, would you?*

Wimbly approached her from behind. He looked about as shocked as she was. "You okay?" he asked.

"Yeah."

"Did I just screw up in there?"

"I don't know," she said, collecting her breath. "Do I have you to thank for this?"

"Maybe a bit. But from here on out, it's all you. And it's both our asses on the line. So let's get to work, like he said."

They walked toward the front doors together but at a slight distance. He opened the front doors for her and when they stepped onto the street, it fully hit Ava like a load of bricks on the head. She'd asked for the case and she'd gotten it. But…now what? A plan came quickly to mind and it seemed deceptively simple.

"So here's my play," Wimbly said as they started walking. "I think we head back to the neighborhood we were in yesterday and talk to some of those club owners. Maybe even some of the families."

"Yes, that sounds good."

"If we strike out there, I've got a list of men that have been busted for trying to run speakeasies that might know a thing or two."

As he spoke, Ava recalled her conversation with Jack yesterday. An idea came to her, but she knew it was not one that Wimbly was going to appreciate.

"I think it should just be me," Ava interrupted.

"Excuse me?"

"You saw Jack Dooley's reaction to you yesterday. He wasn't the only one who feels that way. Any club or club-oriented managers are not going to talk to you. And if they do, they're going to purposefully mislead you and then give you the bum's rush."

"Yes, but you'll be with me. Like yesterday…and that will play to our advantage."

"Possibly. Or the word could get out that I'm now with the police. I do know some of the people in those neighborhoods—people with businesses and some degree of success. If I go traipsing about with a bluenose copper, I'm going to lose their respect and trust. You're a detective…you have to see that, right?"

The look on his face told her that he *did* understand it. But he did not like it at all. "Boy, I just set myself in an awful trap, didn't I?"

"I'll go have a talk with some of the business owners and club-hops at the upscale places. BY myself. It just makes more sense."

"I hate to admit it, but it does. While you do that, I'll talk with the family and friends of the dead women. Two birds, one stone. We'll meet back here in a few hours and compare notes." He let out a heavy breath and added: "Minard will kill me if he knew I let you off on your own."

"I won't tell if you don't," she said jokingly. "Look, I know you did me a solid in there, and I'm not going to make you regret it." Honestly, it was hard to think of Minard in that moment. She was more worried about helping the family and loved ones of the victim—more concerned about making sure no one else died. And if she had to buck the system a bit to get that done, she was fine with that.

"There's no way you were this pushy and bossy with Clarence," Wimbly said. She could tell he meant it as a joke, but there was some resentment there, too.

"About work, absolutely not," she said warmly. "Other things…well," she said, giving a chuckle and shrug.

"Five o'clock," Wimbly said. "You meet me back here at five o'clock. If there's a problem or a lead, you find a phone and call the front desk. If you're more than five minutes late this evening, this is over. I'll go to Minard and tell him you're nothing but a stubborn, self-entitled dame that doesn't take instruction."

"Fair enough," Ava said. She turned away and started walking.

And with her new position and responsibility, the city felt so much larger…and much more dangerous.

CHAPTER THIRTEEN

Ava found doors to Heat Wave open, even at the early hour of 10 o'clock in the morning. The place only held about a hundred people but that was fine; the bigger draw was the speakeasy it ran out of its little attic loft space. It was a little dive of a place with great acoustics. Someone would come in, listen to the music for a few minutes, then sneak upstairs. When they came back down, still bobbing to the music, no one would notice when they left with a bottle or two tucked under their coat. She knew this because she had graced its stage on occasion back when she'd been singing.

She hesitated in front of the doors. Her days as a jazz singer were a little less than two years behind her, but it felt like an eternity. Some of the same streets around those old haunts felt different now. She'd noticed it while on patrol with Frances, but walking alone with her current assignment, it was much more noticeable.

Heat Wave might not be a great place to start looking. A bigger place might have been more promising. There was, of course, the Cotton Club. But no one would be there for several hours. Besides that, she also knew that some very powerful people frequented the Cotton Club—business owners, celebrities, politicians. Ava had never had the privilege of singing there, but had attended a few times. She was no fool; there was no way in hell a freshly minted *woman* detective was going to get any sort of lead out of a place like that.

But Heat Wave was at least open because they also served as a minor hash house on the weekdays. When Ava stepped inside, the place smelled of freshly fried eggs, sizzling meat, and coffee. It was all slightly overpowered by the typical smell of a smaller jazz club: smoke, sweat, and an underlying pungent odor Ava had always associated with brass instruments. There were only two people sitting at the little counter at the front of the place. A man serving as both cook and waiter was rushing out a cup of joe with a plate of eggs.

She did not recognize the cook, which was a shame. The cook/waiter she used to know had been an overweight and joyful black man known only as Bear. The current cook looked to be of Italian descent. She had not been inside Heat Wave in nearly eight months, so she supposed a lot had changed—something that tended to happen in the smaller jazz clubs, thanks to prohibition.

She walked to the bar area and sat down next to one of the two current diners. She was waiting for the cook to come back so she could order a coffee and ask whatever happened to Bear. But before the cook came back, a rusty voice spoke up from beside her.

"Ava?" the man sitting next to her said.

She turned to her right and saw a face that was vaguely familiar. It was one she hadn't seen in nearly three years and back then, it had not been partially covered by the beard she was now looking at. It took a while for the name to come to her, but when it did, she smiled and the name came out almost like a laugh.

"Reggie?"

Reggie Wilson beamed at her. She felt terrible for taking so long to figure out who he was. How many nights had he played his trumpet behind her in this very club and at least a handful of others? Reggie was easily one of the better freelance trumpet players in the city not tied down to any one band so he could enjoy playing with a variety of people. She wasn't sure where he hailed from, but he'd always hinted that his family had been rather privileged in the south following the Civil War. Wanting no part of the racism that had not yet died down that way, he'd come to New York as soon as he could, bringing only a trumpet and some clothes.

"Where on earth did you disappear to, you crazy broad?" Reggie asked.

"Oh, I've always been around. I just took a step away, always planning to come back."

"Oh yeah? And when might that be?"

"Well, it was *going* to be soon…but life sort of took a different direction."

"Oh, I know all about that," Reggie said.

"You're still playing, right?"

"For sure. Playing here tonight with a hotsy-totsy quartet."

The cook came by and Ava ordered her coffee and a biscuit—what Bear had once called a cat-heat biscuit due to its size and shape. She forgot to ask about Bear, though, as she was so wrapped up in catching up with Reggie.

"And what about you?" Reggie asked. "It was the kid, wasn't it? Your kid got older and you needed to be a mom, right? I see it a lot. Mostly women, though. Men apparently don't care."

"Yeah, that was part of it. And I don't regret it."

"Good for you." He frowned and when he looked up, his mood had shifted. "I suppose you're even busier with the kid now, huh? I heard about your husband. I only ever saw him, sitting in the back of clubs you were singing in, but he seemed to really adore you."

"He did. And in terms of what I'm doing now…" She stopped here, wrestling with an unexpected surge of emotion. "I'm sort of trying to fill his shoes."

"You mean, playing the father part, too?"

"No, I mean playing the cop part."

Reggie grinned widely and gave her a perplexed look. "You fooling me?"

"Nope. I'm actually on a case right now. I was hoping to come by and ask Bear some questions because he was always in the know."

"Wow, you haven't been here in a while, have you? Bear got recruited by some hot-shot classy restaurant. He'd been gone for three or four months now. But more importantly…you're really a cop? They have women cops?"

"Sort of. But this one is a special kind of deal…"

"You got a gun?" Reggie asked with a wink.

"No. Nothing like that. I just…hey, wait. You know what? You still get around to all the clubs, right?"

"I do. Some good, some bad, some I'd not even bother mentioning. Why do you ask?"

She was slow to proceed, not wanting to scare him away or make him hesitant to speak with her. "Have you heard about the hatchet killer?"

"Read about it this morning," he said as the cook brought Ava her coffee and biscuit. "That's some scary stuff. They got you looking into it?"

"In a roundabout way, yes. Both of these women are linked to clubs. The one last night was coming home from one when she was killed. The first victim was killed behind the Key Factory. You said you read about it…did you know either of them?"

"The names didn't ring a bell, but I'll tell you this—the way they were killed made me think of this wrong number I always heard about in whispers in the clubs. You ever hear of Tony Two?"

The name didn't ring a bell. "No, I don't think so."

Reggie lowered his head and his voice, clearly enjoying the idea of dishing what he knew. "Tony Two is *literally* a hatchet man. As the story goes, he works for the mob, going around and collecting gambling debts. And that hatchet…that's his gimmick. You're late on a payment, he takes your pinky finger with a hatchet. If that doesn't do the job, he'll come back and take your thumb."

"Who told you about this?" Ava asked.

"No one in particular. It's just some of the stuff you hear, you know? I've seen the guy a time or two—some other players pointed him out to me. A low-level kind of guy. You wouldn't think he'd be that type."

"You've seen him in clubs?" she asked, surprised.

"Just once or twice. But mob guys are coming to shows more and more now—wanting to make their presence known. So it wasn't that big of a deal. Although, you know…one of those places *was* the Key Factory."

"How long ago?" she asked. The case was already showing promise and she hadn't even been on the streets for more than two hours. Was it really going to come together so easily?

"Maybe three months ago. Not sure."

Ava sipped from her coffee and took a bite out of her biscuit, thinking. She reached for her coin purse in her pocket but Reggie protested.

"Nope, I got this, Mrs. Copper. I can see you're on your way out."

"Thanks, Reggie. And look…maybe don't tell anyone what I'm doing these days. Right now, I have the element of surprise working for me."

"You got it…only if you promise to sing with me first when you make your reappearance."

"That's a deal," she said. And she was slightly surprised to realize that she absolutely meant it.

***

As Ava made her way to the Key Factory—which was about three miles away from Heat Wave—she stopped at a few other places she knew. Some, she'd only been in once or twice, and other places felt like home. Like Heat wave, she found that some of the employees she had come to know had either been fired, arrested, or had gone elsewhere. Prohibition was really taking its toll almost everywhere she looked.

She saw two familiar faces along the way—an aging pianist who seemed to barely remember her, and another singer who had often sung as her male accompaniment. The singer's name was Wayland Huston and when Ava ran into him in an up-and-coming clip joint at 1:30, he was giving an informal voice lesson to an eighteen-year-old who, from the sound of it, clearly had talent but needed some fine tuning.

Wayland was happy to see Ava and, like Reggie and Jack Dooley, expressed their sadness that she had stepped away from the scene. When she asked Wayland if he was familiar with a guy known as Tony Two, he got slightly uncomfortable.

"Why are you asking about goons like that, Ava?" he asked. "You know Tony Two is in the mob, right?"

"I do. I just heard some stories and wondered if they were true. I hear the mob is poking their head around more than they used to."

"They are. But I don't really even mind because it means more attention for the clubs and music. But some of these guys—like Tony Two—are just bad news."

"What do you know about him?" she asked

He shared the same information Reggie had given her, but Wayland had a bit more to offer. "Some stool-pigeon was saying Tony got into a heated argument at a club last week. Not sure over what. But from what I hear, his long-time baby doll walked out on him and he's been unhinged ever since. Some people wonder if he doesn't roll up in the clubs with that damned hatchet on him."

Ava wished Wayland well, leaving him to his voice student just twenty minutes after reintroducing herself for the first time in a year and a half. She then finished her circuit, arriving at the Key Factory at three in the afternoon. It should provide her plenty of time to get back to the precinct by five, per Wimbly's orders.

When she walked in the door, she saw some of the night's scheduled musicians already taking their instruments out on the stage, preparing for what she was sure would be a very abbreviated sound check. It made her miss those afternoons, a few secret drinks in her and the afternoon light pouring in through dusty windows and doors as she warmed up for a night's performance. Maybe someday soon, she *would* manage to get back into it.

As she was bathing in the nostalgia of it all, a warm and excited voice greeted her from the far side of the room.

"Ava, I knew you wouldn't stay away so long this time!"

She turned toward Jack Dooley and saw him smoothing out a velvet tablecloth on one of the small tables scattered all over the floor. He slid a chair in behind it and then came over to greet her.

Smiling, he said, "I see you came without the heat today."

"I wasn't *with* him yesterday."

"Well, you should be with him from now on. You being there made him much more likeable!" He shook his head, chuckling, and said: "I still can't believe you're a policeman. Policewoman. What is it? How do I say it?"

"I don't know that it matters. Look, Jack, I have to keep this visit short. Have you heard about the other woman that was killed?"

"No! Who was it?"

"A woman named Annie Tate. Does that sound familiar to you?"

Jack considered it for a moment and then shook his head. "Can't say it does. You think it was the same guy that offed the woman in my alleyway?"

"It looks that way. And that's why I'm here. I think I might have a lead. What do you know about a mobster by the name of Tony Two?"

"You're not going after *him*, are you?" Jack asked, aghast.

"No," she said, though she really had no idea what the rest of the day would bring. "I've just been putting a profile together on him today. You know who he is?"

"I do, oh yeah. Creepy little goon, that's for sure. Not that I'd ever tell him. The mob...you can never be too careful, you know."

"How well do you know him?"

"Not well. Just from what folks have told me. He's been in here a few times. Never started trouble but everyone sort of stayed away from him, you know. Except the ladies he brought in with him."

"I suppose you know what they say he does for the mob?"

"Yeah. Takes fingers if you owe money. And if you ask me, if you can do that sort of thing, there ain't much else you won't do."

"Is there anything about him you can tell me that hasn't already been whispered about?"

Jack looked to the ground and frowned. He opened his mouth and then closed it, looking back up at Ava and clearly wrestling with something.

"It's okay, Jack. You can tell me. Your name will stay out of it."

"There was this guy that used to come in here a while back...almost every Monday and Wednesday night. A big gambler-type. He's a real whiz at poker from what I gather. He always bragged that he's played 'em all. Even some mobsters. He said that when the mobsters go out for some fun, they sometimes bring him along to win some cash. He said sometimes he plays with some mob guys on Thursday nights. He even named a few...and one of them was Tony Two. That's apparently how he got his name; he's really lucky with the deuces."

"Thursdays," Ava said. "So...tonight. You know where they play?"

"Ava…I can't. I can't send you into it. And if they find out it was me…"

"I'd never do that to you, Jack. Between you and me…there are a lot of eyes on me. If I fail and make men angry, I can live with that. But a young woman is dead—two, in fact. And I want to make sure there won't be any more. Also, the last thing I'd want to do in trying to prove myself is make a mark out of old friends."

Jack nodded and would not look at her when he answered. "It's a backroom poker game. Takes place pretty much all night. Cards, drinking, women, sort of a party from what I hear. They have it out of the back of that small auto dealership on Madison."

"You're sure of this?" Ava asked. She could hardly believe her luck—how reliable her old friends were turning out to be.

"Oh yeah…this fool was so proud of himself, he told every single detail he could."

"Thanks, Jack."

"Sure. Now as payment, you need to get up on my stage sometime soon."

She was flattered; it was the second such invitation she'd gotten today. The thought was almost as exciting as the information she'd just gotten—a strong lead to a mobster known to use hatchets on people.

She tried to seem confident and calm as she left, but when she hit the streets, she put a bit of extra speed into her step, anxious to tell Frank Wimbly she might be on to something. But more than that, the extra bounce in her step was a great way to convince herself she wasn't as nervous as she actually was. In a way, she supposed she might be trying to outrun the sense of foreboding she was starting to feel, creeping up behind her.

CHAPTER FOURTEEN

When Ava returned to the precinct at 4:55 that afternoon, Frank was nowhere to be found. She didn't want to go into the building in search of him because if Minard found out, there might be hell to pay. She walked the block a few times, meandering through the thickening afternoon activity on the streets, but Frank never showed up. When her watch read 5:20, she figured it was worth taking a chance.

She headed inside and found that the precinct had calmed considerably since this morning. Still, she assumed Minard was holed up somewhere looking into the hatchet killer case. She hurriedly approached the front desk and did her best to put on an embarrassed look. She found Wayne Gibb standing behind it. He looked a little flustered as she approached.

"Hello, Mr. Gibb," she said. "I was wondering if there were any messages for me from Detective Wimbly."

Gibb looked down to the desk and thumbed through a few sheets of paper before shaking his head. "Nothing."

She feigned confusion and leaned on the desk. "He was onto a lead and asked me to come back to the station. But I haven't seen him since we separated. So…I guess I need to leave one for him."

Gibb picked up a pen and nodded to her to go ahead.

"Possible break at the auto dealership on Madison."

Gibb jotted it down and said, "That's it?"

"Yes, thanks, Mr. Gibb."

Although things felt incomplete and up in the air, she finished out her day as expected. She finished up some of the paperwork from the welcome packet that had gone neglected, enjoying the secure feeling of sitting behind the desk down in the office of the Women's Bureau. When all of that was done, she quickly headed back outside just to make sure she would not accidentally run into Minard. Besides, there was still so sign of Frank, so she thought it seemed like a waste of time to just stay around the precinct.

She thought of the poker game that would be taking place on Madison later tonight. She toyed with the idea of calling the precinct and dropping the clue to Minard. It seemed like the smart thing to do on the surface, but she doubted anyone would take her lead seriously.

Also, even if it *was* taken seriously, Minard and all others further up the ladder would demand to know where she got her information—and she wasn't about to offer up old friends like that.

It was 5:55 when she reached the gym. She found the door closed and locked. Her dad usually stayed open until seven; she wondered what was different about today. Wondering if Jeffrey was maybe sick or had gotten into some sort of trouble at school, she hurried home.

Her feet were aching by the time she got to her apartment. She wondered how much longer these shoes would last and made a mental note to set some money aside from an extra pair just in case. She was thinking of how to even start setting money aside when she got to her apartment. She could smell food cooking on the other side—biscuits baking and the smell of some sort of meat.

She entered to find her father and Jeffrey at the stove. The biscuits had just come out of the oven, and the meat that was cooking was bacon, sizzling and popping on the burner. She also saw that a tomato had been sliced up. From the lopsided size and cut of the slices, she assumed this had been Jeffrey's contribution.

"Dad, I was actually on time today," Ava said as she closed the door behind her. "Why'd you close early?"

"My one lesson cancelled on me for the day," Roosevelt said. "And Jeffrey here was getting bored, so we left."

"Bored at the boxing gym?" Ava said, leaning in to kiss her son on the cheek.

"Well," Roosevelt said, "that, and I was hungry. Now stop interrogating us and set the table, would you?"

The three of them sat down to a dinner of bacon and tomato biscuits—a simple dinner that Jeffrey had always loved. And while Roosevelt's biscuits were dense and dry, she loved that Jeffrey was polite enough not to complain. As they ate, Ava did what she could to keep all conversation geared toward Jeffrey's school and what was currently going on at the gym.

"Any promising kids down at the gym these days?" she asked.

"Oh yeah, for sure," Roosevelt said, his eyes lighting up. "I've got this nineteen-year-old who used to work the docks...he's got fists like iron mallets and feet like a dancer. Another three months of training and he might have a legitimate shot at some real fighters."

She was glad to see him excited because it got Jeffrey excited, even though he did not yet understand the full scope of professional boxing. And anything that kept Jeffrey alight and smiling these days was always welcome.

With dinner over, Roosevelt willingly cleaned the dishes while Ava and Jeffrey headed to his bedroom. While he changed into pajamas, Ava sat down on his floor and looked through his thin collection of books. She picked one out and said, "What about *The Lucky Pup*?"

Jeffrey frowned but said, "Sure. That's fine."

"Do you not want a story?" Ava asked.

"Not one of those. I want one like Dad used to tell."

Ava felt her heart shudder a bit. Her palms started to grow sweaty right away and an idea came to her. "Jeffrey, I'm never going to be able to tell those stories like your father could. But you know what? What about I tell you a story *about* your dad? There sure are enough of them to choose from."

"Whoa, really? That would be great!"

They sat on his bed and as she began Jeffrey settled his head into her shoulder. "Now, you know your dad didn't get upset very easily," Ava started, "but that wasn't true on the day he had to go scare off all these stray dogs that found their way into a butcher's shop."

Jeffrey was giggling right away, and it helped her to get though the story. Because even though it was absolutely a true story—and among the funniest she'd ever heard from Clarence and his friends alike—it made her miss him fiercely. When the story was over ten minutes later, Ava could not decide if the tears streaming down her face were of joy or sorrow.

She tucked Jeffrey in and gave him a kiss goodnight. He'd been going to bed much earlier since Clarence died and when she closed his door, she thought it looked like he was already nodding off.

She found her father in the living room, thumbing through her records. She found this funny, as he'd always been quite vocal about how much he disliked jazz. He enjoyed what he called "hillbilly music" from artists like Uncle Dave Macon and Jimmie Rodgers.

"Still nothing good to listen to," Roosevelt commented as she came into the room.

"That's a matter of opinion," Ava said, settling down into her favorite chair. "Thanks for dinner, Dad. You didn't have to."

"I know. But I wanted to. You've got this high-falutin' job now. You need all the help you can get. How's it going, by the way?"

The little girl wanting to please her father was bursting to tell him that she'd been assigned a case. But the facts of it all would suck the joy out of it—that she was only on it to paint a pretty picture of the police force in the wake of what was looking to turn into a serial killer case.

"There's a lot of walking, that's for sure."

"Are the men down there giving you hell? Need me to give them a talking to?"

She thought of the man who had tried to assault her in the locker room, and the reactions of the men who had come in with him. "I'm getting some sass, but nothing too bad. I'm a big girl, Dad."

"Oh, I know. A big girl with a vicious right hook, at that." He cracked his knuckles nervously and looked sadly at his daughter. "Ava, I've been thinking about it and…if you'll have me, I'd like to stay here for a while. I think it'll just be easier until you get used to the job and until you and Jeffrey both get used to Clarence not being here."

"That's lovely, Dad, but where would you sleep?"

"I'll lug the mattress from my apartment."

Ava wriggled her nose at the thought of the grimy apartment over the gym—the place he'd been calling home for more than ten years now, ever since her mother had died. She was about to comment on his apartment and the aforementioned mattress, but then a thought occurred to her. With the thought came guilt, and then a bit of excitement.

"You know," she said, "you could start tonight, if you want. There was a small case at work that I was asked to help with after hours but I didn't know how you'd feel about it—and I had told Jeffrey I'd be on time this evening. If you want to stay here tonight, you could have my bed and I'll bunk with Jeffrey when I get back."

"Really? What sort of case do they have dames working on after hours?"

"I think it's just some records stuff…looking into these two recent murders of women."

The lie came too easy—as did the thought of Clarence's gun resting on the top shelf of their bedroom closet.

"I'm game for it if you are," Roosevelt said. "You sure your old man living with you isn't going to get in the way?"

"Of course not," she said, getting to her feet and giving him a hug. "I love having you around. And I think it helps Jeffrey more than you know."

"You leaving *now*?" he asked.

"Yeah. The sooner I leave, the sooner I'll get back. Just need to change my clothes."

This was another lie. *They seem to really be piling up, huh?* she thought.

She knew she was lying because the idea she had seemed a little crazy. Now, thinking of the old Smith and Wesson Model 10 Clarence kept in their closet, she couldn't help but *not* think of her plan.

She went to the bedroom and walked toward the closet. She thought of Jeffrey and of how careful she needed to be when she went out. But more than that, she thought of a man known as Tony Two—and how he wasn't going to be at this poker game forever.

CHAPTER FIFTEEN

The streets were lit up by a few glowering street lamps as Ava made her way over toward Madison Avenue. It was nearing nine o'clock and there weren't many people on the street. On her way over, she paused outside of a public telephone booth, wondering if she should call the precinct to see if Frank had ever showed up and left a message for her. It seemed like a bad idea, though; if it was discovered she'd called at this hour looking for Frank, it would *really* seem that they had been working independently and that she had already gone way off the rails.

She turned her back on the phone and continued walking as the intersection that would cross her over to the automobile dealership came into view. She walked slowly, as to not draw attention from anyone she passed. She knew she likely looked a little out of place because she was wearing a thin cardigan jacket despite the modest heat of the summer night. The cardigan was necessary though, as it was hiding the pistol that was tucked between her back and the waistband of her skirt.

As the auto dealership came into view, she tried talking herself out of going ahead. She had a child at home. She had a future head of her, even if Clarence was no longer here. Did she really think she was just going to drop in on a mobster's poker game and get all the answers she needed for this case?

She didn't know. But what she did know was that her knees were already deciding for her, working in tandem with her feet to haul her across the street. She looked to the darkened glass of the dealership. There were others in town that were doing much better as people started to make more money and realized just how reliable and necessary automobiles would be in the coming years. There were even projections that half the county would be using them by the 1950s—something that seemed almost unreal to Ava. However, the one on Madison was a newer one and, as far as she knew, wasn't doing quite as well as the others. Given that, she supposed it made sense for the owner to allow illegal poker games involving nefarious men on his property. Certainly there was some sort of financial advantage to it.

She stayed a good distance away after crossing the street. She remained out of the building's shadow until she had walked all the way around to the back. If she needed proof that Jack Dooley had been telling her the truth, she saw it in the form of three parked cars in the rear lot. There was a single door along the back wall of the building and as she approached it, she could see a little sliver of light along the bottom, barely touching the parking lot.

Ava walked to the door and pressed her ear against it. She could hear several murmuring voices and muted movement. Someone coughed lightly, then two people laughed. She thought she even heard a woman's faint voice as well.

Slowly, she tried the door and was rather surprised to find that it was not locked. She guessed anyone with information about this game would have had an invitation—so there was no need to lock the door. With the knob already halfway turned in her hands, she figured she may as well go ahead and get the job done. She took a deep breath, steeled up her courage, and pushed the door open.

At the same time, she stepped inside and pulled out the S&W Model 10. The world went swimmy for just a moment, mainly because of the almost natural feeling that swept through her as she drew the weapon.

As she stepped inside and the door swung closed behind her, the world seemed to freeze for a moment. Ava found herself looking at a rather small, crowded room. There were four men in the room, sitting around a small table set up in the center of the floor. One of the men had a long-legged dame sitting on his knee. Another man was also paired with a broad who had gams that seemed to go straight up to her neck. She was currently leaning over, pretending to get a good look at the cards but really just shoving her sample bosom into the man's face in an obvious way. The room was filled with smoke and the strong yet enticing smell of liquor.

"What the…" one of the men said as all eyes turned to Ava.

She saw the man known as Tony Two, slightly shorter than the rest, but dressed very dapper. There was a hesitant smile on his face as he tried to figure out why this crazy dame had burst in on his poker game. The other men had the same look on their faces but then, all at once, they seemed to notice the gun in her hands.

Questions flew through the air like bullets as everyone suddenly snapped to a crazy sort of attention.

"What are you doing with that bean shooter?" one of the men asked.

"Who the hell are you?" one of the others asked.

Tony Two, getting to his feet and reaching toward his waist asked, "What are you doing here, you crazy skirt?"

"Keep your hands where I can see them, Tony."

Tony's eyes narrowed when she used his name. He hesitated and stopped moving his hands. The other men also got to their feet, their ladies backing away to the far wall.

"This some kind of raid?" Tony asked. He snickered here and grinned, looking to his boys. When he looked back to Ava he said, "You some kind of cop?"

Everyone laughed at this, even the women.

"As a matter of fact, yes," Ava said. "And no, this isn't a raid. This is—"

She barely saw the man to the right move. He moved very fast, pelting a brown bottle at her. Clear, pungent-smelling liquid came spilling out of it as it flew end over end toward her. Ava dodged the bottle just in time; she could hear it whistling past her ear and got splashes of the alcohol in her hair.

While she was distracted, Tony went back to his waist, surely about to pull a gun. Ava pivoted out of her dodge and wheeled back around with a backhanded blow. It took Tony in the chest and he stumbled backwards. He *had* been going for a gun—it clattered to the floor as she struck him.

As he reached for it, one of the women at the back had apparently had enough of this scene. She dashed forward, heading for the door In her haste, her elegantly crafted leg slammed into Tony Two's head just as he grabbed the gun. Ava took advantage of this and dashed forward, gun still raised.

"Stand up, Tony!"

Tony did as she asked, looking at her as if he might very well shoot bullets out of his eyes. Ava wasn't sure anyone had ever looked at her with so much anger before. As they locked eyes, another of the poker players took advantage and, in an act of desperation, flipped the table over. Cards, money, and cigars went flying. More alcohol was spilled, and the back room of the auto dealership was suddenly alive with a flurry of activity.

The table struck Ava's legs and she stumbled back. One of the other men came rushing after her, his eyes on her gun. Ava did not want to use it—not at all, actually—so she quickly transferred it to her left hand so she could catch the man with a vicious jab to the chin. It rocked him hard and he staggered back, his eyes going swimmy as he fell.

As soon as he fell, another man was coming after her, As he did, she noted two other things: the third man was going for Tony's gun and Tony was scrambling for the door, right behind the woman with the generous bosom.

She acted quickly, figuring she had about three seconds before the third man had the gun in his hands and took aim. She brought her own gun up, hating how odd it felt in her left hand. It was enough to get the rushing man to stop, though. With his eyes distracted by the sight of the pistol, she brought her right hand around again, cold-cocking him right along the temple. He spun in a half circle, tripped on one of the table legs, and went down in a heap.

Ava then placed her foot on the upended table and pushed hard at it. She pushed it against the man going for Tony's gun and the leg closest to him slammed into his shoulder. As he reeled back from that attack, Ava grabbed Tony's gun and turned to stop him from retreating.

But it was too late. Tony had already made his way out the door and across the parking lot. She could just barely see his dark form turning to nothing more than shadow as he sprinted across the corner and down Madison. In his retreat, he'd knocked down one of the women from the back room. She was still on the ground, holding her forearm to her chest. Ava instinctively reached down to help her up, her eyes still on Tony's retreating figure.

As she watched, she saw another figure come hurtling out of the shadows of one of the neighboring buildings, on a collision course with Tony Two.

"What the hell…" Ava said.

She took off running, releasing the slender woman so quickly that she almost fell to the pavement again. Ava ran as hard as she could, now transferring the pistol back to her right hand. She kept her eyes on the two figures as they came together and as they tumbled, it was clear to see that someone had come from out of nowhere to knock Tony Two down.

It wasn't until she was about a dozen or so feet away that she clearly saw the other figure.

It was Frank. He had Tony Two down on the concrete and was applying handcuffs. Frank looked up to Ava and said, "I damn sure hope there's a need for me putting these things on."

"He drew a gun on me…or, rather, tried."

"Crazy broad!" Tony yelled as Frank hauled him to his feet. "What's this all about anyway?"

Ava and Frank ignored him. Frank looked in the direction Ava and Tony had been coming from and frowned slightly. "Were you chasing him or something? I got your note about the auto dealership…"

"I sort of was. There's three other guys back there."

"They hurt you? Are they still there?"

She shrugged almost playfully. "Oh, they're still there, all right."

"Crazy broad came in just throwing punches with that bean shooter pulled out!" Tony said.

"Hold on," Frank said, marching Tony along with them as they hurried back to the dealership. "You mean to tell me you busted up a poker game and beat up four men on your own?"

"I wouldn't say *beat up*," Ava said.

They came to the door and Ava opened it slowly. One of the men was getting back to his feet, using the wall as leverage. The other two were still knocked out cold.

Frank turned to her with a confused smile—an *impressed* smile, if Ava was reading it correctly. "If you don't call this *beat up*, I sure would like to know what you call it."

"How much trouble is this going to put me in?"

With the same smile on his face, Frank shook his head. "If you can start showing some of this side at the station, I'll make sure there's no trouble."

"Oh, I can make it enough for you," Tony said.

"That sounds like a threat, Tony Two," Frank said. "I think we need to have a little chat at the station."

CHAPTER SIXTEEN

"I ain't no rat," Tony said as they hauled him into the precinct. Ava was directly behind him and the automatic attention the man generated made her slightly uncomfortable. He spoke loudly, as if wanting to make sure he gave everyone on duty a show. "And I didn't do a damned thing tonight."

"Tell it to us in an interrogation room," Frank said, pushing him roughly along. Ava could tell Frank wanted to get the guy to an interrogation room before he caused too much chaos and confusion in the bullpen and hallways of the station.

"Why you being so rough with me?" Tony demanded. "Being tough now, I see. But it was this dame right here that did all the work!" He cackled as he got more and more attention, officers turning in his direction as he was marched through the building. "You coppers hear that? This big bad copper didn't do a thing but tackle me when I wasn't looking! It was the broad that had the real muscle!"

Frank sneered and hauled Tony all the way back to the interrogation rooms. When Ava followed him in, she realized it was her fist time inside of one. Honestly, when she'd asked Minard for the job, she never dreamed she would have come this far—and especially not in such record time. It was awe-inspiring, but it also made her feel as if all of the weight of the world was, in that moment, on her shoulders.

The room contained only a table and two chairs, one on each side. Simple and straightforward, but to Ava it felt like the site of some huge test. And she was the only one taking it.

Frank shoved Tony into the chair on the opposite side of the table with such force that it, and Tony along with it, almost went tipping over.

"You done screaming?" Frank asked.

"What's wrong, dick? I embarrass you?"

Ava could see the fury in Frank's eyes when he turned to her. He did his best to keep his voice calm and calculated when he spoke. "Officer Gold, would you step out and let me talk to this gentleman?"

Ava nodded. She was a bit disappointed, but given the way the night had gone she didn't want to push too hard.

"No way, copper," Tony said. He eyed them both, a smile growing wide on his face. "I got no clue what you even want to talk about, but I'm not saying a word to anyone but her." He nodded at Ava when he said this and she could tell by the arrogant smile still on his face that he thought he was working the situation to his advantage by making such a request.

"No deal," Frank said.

Tony shrugged and crossed his arms. "Then go ahead and find your horse shit charges to press against me. But I know how this game works, oh yes I do. This broad comes in waving a gun around and cold-cocks some unarmed men. Then you tackle me, unprovoked. And let's be real. You know about some of my connections, right? I can make this look bad for not just you, but the whole station. Hell, all of the NYPD. And with that killer on the loose…damn, that would look awful bad, huh?"

Ava watched as Frank turned away from Tony. She could see the restraint in the muscles of his forearm and the tightly locked set of his chin. With his back still turned to Tony, he said, "Fine. Then talk."

Tony nodded to the chair across from his, as if he had just invited his best girl out for dinner. "What brought you to my poker game tonight?" Tony asked.

Ava knew he did not intend to make this easy—that he was just playing a part to annoy Frank. But she could play that game, too. As arrogant as it made her feel, she already knew she had impressed him with her fighting skills tonight. If she could somehow stay in that zone, she'd be golden.

"A tip from someone," she said.

"What kind of tip? Be careful now. Not many people know about that poker game. If I really wanted to, I could ask around and find out who told you. I could make some trouble for them."

"Oh, I don't doubt it. Your reputation…well, it's getting around. Hatchet and all." This seemed to not sit well with Tony, so she forged ahead quickly before the comment had time to simmer. "Tony, I honestly don't give a damn what sort of things you're doing with the mob these days. Booze, women, roughing folks up…I don't care."

"You expect me to believe that?"

"Do or don't…no skin off my backside. No. There's a bigger game, here. You mentioned that killer we're looking for just a few seconds ago. And that's funny…because we *are* still looking for him. And you just happen to be our primary suspect."

The grin slid off Tony's face so fast it looked like his face was melting. "You kidding me, sweetheart?"

"No. And don't call me sweetheart."

It was clear that Tony Two was not used to being spoken to this way. She watched his face go through a variety of emotions. When it settled on anger for a moment, she understood how he might strike fear into people despite his small stature.

"What's wrong, Tony?" Ava asked.

"You mean aside from being read the third degree by some uppity broad?"

"Yes, aside from that."

She saw what she assumed passed for sincerity settle into his features. His posture relaxed slightly and his eyes softened. "Let's be real. You guys likely know a bit about me, yeah? I've done some things that aren't exactly...*polite*. But I draw the line at hurting women. A man that hurts a woman is the worst sort of man on the earth. Believe it or not, it's a common way of life with a lot of the men I work with. There's just some things you don't do."

"I respect that, naturally," Ava said. The entire tone of the conversation had shifted with Tony's admission, so she figured she may as well strike while the iron was hot. But she also doubted the sincerity of this. After all, one of his low-life friends had thrown a beer bottle at her. Still, she played her part and said: "And if you can give us some details of your whereabouts on the night these two women were killed, you're free to go."

She sensed Frank tensing up behind her at this comment, but chose to ignore it for the moment.

"When was it?" he asked.

"The most recent was just last night. The first was two days ago."

Tony shifted uncomfortably in his seat. She could see him thinking through several things as his very expressive face settled on a frown. "I can't tell you that."

"And why not?"

"Because I'd be snitching on some people. And, like not hitting women, we don't tend to rat our friends out."

"With all due respect," Ava said, "I don't buy this not-hitting-women crap. We know the sort of men you associate with. I can easily remember a beer bottle being chucked at my head."

Tony shrugged and said, "Hey, I didn't throw it."

Ava considered this for a moment before saying, "Can't you tell us what we need to know without revealing the names of the people you were with?"

Tony Two actually considered it for a moment and then shook his head. "Sorry, no. I can't run that chance."

"I don't guess it would matter if we said we wouldn't follow up on anything that sounds suspicious unless it was related to these murders, would it?"

"Sorry," he said. And as odd as it seemed, Ava was pretty sure he meant it.

Frank stepped forward and when he did, Ava was glad to see his demeanor had changed. "That's fine," he said. "But you get that we can't just let you go right now, right? Not unless you can give us an alibi of some kind."

"Yeah, I get that." He then sat back in his chair, as if he wasn't at all bothered by it.

Frank looked to Ava and said, "Can we have a word outside?"

They left the interrogation room, closing the door on Tony Two. Frank walked a few steps away from the door and leaned against the wall, his arms crossed at his chest.

"I think he did it," Frank said.

"Based on what?" Ava asked.

"For starters, his refusal to tell us where he was when these women were killed."

"I get that, but if he's with the mob, doesn't that sort of make sense?" She recalled several times when Clarence had come home, griping about how certain members of the mob were basically untouchable. Not only that, but they were thick as thieves and never turned on one another. If *she* knew that, then surely Frank knew it. "What about what he said about not hurting women? Is that like a standing rule among mobsters?"

"I don't know." He zoned out into thought for a moment and then shrugged. "I do have to admit that no cases come immediately to mind where monsters have killed women. Some abuse their wives, and it's always kept quiet. So…I don't know."

"The let me ask you this," Ava said. "Let's say we keep him on suspicion…that he ends up in a cell. How long until the mob starts to poke their nose into it all after they find out Tony Two is in the cooler for two murders, but without any evidence?"

"I don't know," he said again, a little bitter and angry this time. "But for right now, it's the only play we have—a play *you* kicked into gear when you stormed into that poker game by yourself. So right now, we stick with this while we keep looking into the case—for evidence that Tony did it or otherwise."

With that, Frank turned around and stormed off toward the bullpen—maybe back home for all Ava knew. Meanwhile, she could only turn and look at the closed door of the interrogation room, haunted by the fact that she was fairly certain the man on the other side was innocent. Sure, she was new to all of this but she'd head Clarence talk about how to read people. And based on what she'd taken from his stories, she just didn't think Tony Two was being defensive enough. He was more worried about potentially squealing on men in his inner circle than he was that he was under suspicion of murder. It just didn't feel right to her.

CHAPTER SEVENTEEN

His mother's voice was louder than ever. It was like the old nag was in the next room, screaming at him through the walls.

You were almost seen last time, you moron, she said. *My God, you give yourself into these sick impulses and can't even do that right.*

He sat in the small armchair his mother had died in. He was rubbing his head, sensing a headache coming on, thinking about the therapies he'd endured back at the hospital. Had they really helped at all, or had they made it worse?

They should have kept you there, his mother's voice said. *Should have done some of that electric shock stuff to you to fry that sad little brain of yours. God, you're pathetic.*

He sprang out of the armchair as if something had bitten him. He started pacing the living room, his breath coming in harsh, labored sounds. He knew his mother was nowhere in the house. She'd been buried in the city, in one of the random cemeteries scattered around one of the useless churches. He wasn't sure which one. He hadn't attended the funeral. Still, he stared at the wall, fearful of whatever she might say next.

He supposed he could leave the city. It was too damn crowded and those women were *everywhere.* Maybe if he headed somewhere down south where farmland and open fields were still everywhere, maybe then his head would sort itself out.

That's right, his mother moaned from the other room. *Run away from your problems. No need to face them like a man...*

He screamed and headed for the door. He stepped outside into a reasonably cool afternoon and felt a momentary sense of relief. The fresh air and the sun were like a cleansing agent, washing the noise of his mother's voice out of his head. He walked with his head down, as it seemed to slowly push away the headache he'd felt growing behind his eyes.

He walked and thought of his mother, of killing her and wandering the streets until he was placed in the hospital. It was all a blur, really, but he had never bothered to question it. He recalled a faint face hovering above him, that of a policeman, and then a doctor. And then came the beds and the painful treatments, and the train of drugs. No one had ever made the connection between his mother's death and his wandering the streets. It had all just sort of vanished, and the only thing left behind was the pestering voice that often erupted in his head.

Somehow, these hazy thoughts had brought him to the city streets. They were familiar streets, avenues and lanes he'd walked countless times in the past few months. He paused for a moment, not quite sure how he'd arrived there. Night was beginning to fall and something about that was also a relief. The night spoke of unseen things, of shadow and secrets. He smiled, despite his unease.

Women were everywhere. Many were on the arms of men. Some walked alone, perhaps shopping or visiting with friends. Some were pretty and some were plain. Others—only a few here and there—were so beautiful that it made no real sense to him. Perfect faces, nice bright eyes, breasts hidden by their clothes but perfect all the same, the way they walked, the way they smelled…

Ah, but there was power there, too. And that was what often sent his heart into a rage.

He stopped in front of a small tobacco shop and watched a woman across the street. He spied her through an opened apartment window. She was doing something with the curtains, straightening them or dusting them, he wasn't sure. Her chin was nice and angular, her mouth a perfect red curve that was nonchalantly smiling. The summer air came through the window and barely brushed her hair.

He was walking toward the building before he was fully aware of what he was doing. He was so transfixed by the sight of the woman in the window that he almost walked right in front of a car. He jumped back with a sneer. There were too many of those damned cars in the streets now. What the hell kind of world was this becoming anyway?

With his heart hammering, he stepped back onto the street. He looked back up to the window where the woman had been, but she had moved on to some other chore. And though she was gone, the urge was not. It thrummed like a hot wire right through his heart and he wasn't sure he'd ever be able to escape it—though he honestly did not want to.

***

Theresa's mother had warned her about taking the job at such an early age. She'd told her about the sort of men that "those clubs" attracted and the trouble that came with them. Theresa supposed her mother had been right, but then again, her mother had no idea the sort of money she made.

Sure, she was just a cigarette girl at the Big Riff, but for an eighteen-year-old young woman to make this sort of scratch…it was sort of unheard of. All she had to endure were older drunk men calling her "baby doll" and "sweet thing," as well as the occasional squeeze on her ass. And for that inconvenience, she had more cash tucked into the front of her shirt for one night's work than her mother would make all of next week.

And when she'd put the trays away and started for the doors to go home, a *very* intoxicated man had come up to her, hugged her just tight enough to press her breasts against his chest, and thanked her for her hard work—whatever that meant. And for that alone, he'd passed a crisp dollar bill her way. In his drunken stupor, he'd even offered to walk her home. She declined, though she loved the idea of what her mother would say if a fifty-something drunken gentleman escorted her little girl home.

The thought of this put a smile on Theresa's face as she headed home. The night was quite beautiful, right after midnight when the summer nights carry a coolness that, in her opinion, rivaled even the nicest of breezes on cooler mornings.

She had a seven-block walk home, and though she'd made it many times before, she'd only covered it at this time of night three times before. This was the first time, though, that she'd been walking with thirty-two bucks stuffed securely into her brassiere. Theresa was busy thinking about how to present the money to her mother (did she gloat, or offer her mother a bit to help pay for this month's utilities?) when a man's voice called out to her from the right.

"Hey, there," was all the voice said.

She turned and saw a man coming out of an alley between two small apartment buildings. "Hello," she said in a low voice, mainly because she'd been raised with the instruction to never be rude to anyone.

"It's awful late, little girl," the man said. "I can walk you home if you want."

"No thank you."

She thought that was the end of it but then he started moving. She was also quite sure he was muttering something under his breath.

"Oh, not like that," the man said with a laugh. He stepped out of the alley and slowly walked slightly behind her. "I'm not one of those men. Honest. I just know how things can be in this city and want to make sure pretty girls like you aren't in danger."

"I'm fine, thanks," Theresa said, now a little nervous as the man continued to follow her.

Again, that muttering came out of his throat. It was like he was having a conversion with himself while also trying to keep tabs on her. She suddenly wished she'd taken the drunk man up on his offer to walk her home.

"Ah, come on," he said, his tone chipper now that he was no longer mumbling.

"I'm okay," she said, a bit more stern now. "My home is right up here at—"

He moved quickly. Before she knew it, he was no longer behind her. He was right beside her. He was reaching out and grabbing her shoulder. It was not the playful or appreciative sort of groping she'd experienced all night at the Big Riff. There was danger in this man's grasp and she knew it before he even clamped down on her shoulder. Even worse, though, was the odd chattering noise he made. She was quite certain he was talking under his breath. She recognized the word "mother" but that was about it.

She felt him trying to pull her backwards, likely back to the alley he had come out of. Acting just as quickly as he had, Theresa spun hard to the left and shrugged her shoulder out of his grip. She wasted no time hurrying forward down the street. Within two sprinting steps, one of her pumps came flying off of her feet and clattered to the sidewalk.

She glanced behind her and saw that he was coming after her. She saw parts of his face in the shadows of night. He was smiling—he was by God *smiling* as he came chasing after her and there was something about his smile that was scarier than any imagined thing he might do to her if he caught her.

And even still, he kept murmuring under his breath. "…won't you, Mother? If you just…"

She opened her mouth to scream for help, but as it turned out, she didn't need to. There were two men standing on the corner up ahead. One was smoking a cigar and they were both looking at her running forward. When their eyes fell on the man behind her, they both started forward.

"He bothering you, ma'am?" one of them asked.

"Yes! Yes, he tried to—"

But before she could explain herself, the men took off running. They came running in her direction and then passed her. When she turned around to see what was happening, she saw that the man who had come out of the alleys had retreated. The men who had potentially saved her life were chasing after him, trying to make sure he did not get away.

But within a few seconds it became clear to Theresa, and to the kind men as well, that the man was just too fast. He'd already slipped down a side street and was out of sight. The man with the cigar still draping out of the corner of his mouth approached her with caution in his eyes.

"Are you all right, little lady?" he asked.

Theresa nodded and started to cry.

"Come on now, then," he said as his friend joined him. "Let us make sure you get home."

This time, Theresa said yes.

CHAPTER EIGHTEEN

When Ava walked into the door of the Women's Bureau, most of the women applauded. Lottie in particular seemed to be very involved. She even let out one of those high-pitched whistles using her fingers that men often used for women walking down the street. Frances sat at her desk, rolling her eyes at the display, but there was satisfaction on her face as well.

Ava shook her head, but it was hard to contain her smile. "There's no need for all of that," she said.

"Um, excuse me," Lottie said. "The story going around the precinct is that you handed four men their asses last night, and you did it all without Frank Wimbly's help."

"I got lucky," Ava said. She knew it was partially true, but she also didn't want to soak up the adulation. It was a rule her father had taught her at the boxing gym. *When people start praising a fighter, they get confident, They get cocky, and they go soft. And then when that knock-out punch comes for their heads, it hurts all the worse when you gotta pick yourself back up.*

"When you've got Tony Two—an admitted member of the mob with a pretty violent streak—yelling that you're a hell of a fighter, that's more than luck," another of the women said. It was one of the women who had not spoken to her on her first few days. Apparently last night's events had changed her tune.

"Whatever the case," Frances said, "the important thing is that you were given the opportunity to close the hatchet-killer case and you did. Nabbed a killer and made the streets safer. That's the important thing."

"What?" Ava said. "Who said he was the killer?"

"Pretty much everyone," Frances said. "Why? What's going on?"

"I don't really know," Ava said. "Excuse me, ladies."

She left the WB offices and headed back upstairs. She was headed for Minard's office to find out what the status of the hatchet-killer case really was when she caught sight of Frank coming across the bullpen. She also noticed some of the men laughing behind their hands as he walked by them.

Frank caught up to her when she was just a few steps away from Minard's office. Remaining as professional as he could, Frank said, "Officer Gold, a word, please?"

She nodded as he led her to what she assumed was his desk. It sat slightly off to the side of the bullpen. It was cluttered with a few opened files and looked somehow more prestigious than the smaller desks located in the central bullpen area. She stood at the edge with her arms folded as Frank sat behind the desk. When he spoke, he did so quietly, as if he were terrified the other officers might hear them talking.

"Listen," he said. "I know you had nothing to do with all that stuff Tony Two was spouting when we brought him in here. But enough people heard it in the station that it's making the rounds. I trust you're an honest woman, and I'd appreciate it if you didn't do anything to add fuel to the fire."

"I'd never do anything like that," she said. Honestly, she was a little offended he'd assumed she'd even think of such a thing.

"I figured you wouldn't. I just wanted to come to an understanding."

"Of course. Now, speaking of an understanding, I want to know why everyone is saying we have our killer. We never came an agreement that Tony Two was the hatchet killer."

Frank shrugged and looked nervously around the precinct. "You're right. We didn't. And if I'm being honest with you, I'm not sure myself. But the reality of the situation is that it fits. After you left last night, Captain Minard asked if I thought Tony was the killer. I told him I thought it was a very strong possibility that Tony Two was our guy, but it wasn't a certainty."

"So where is he?"

"Tony? He's in a holding cell."

"But he didn't do it."

"You don't know that," Frank said, slightly annoyed. "There's no reason to make this harder than it has to be. Right now, we have someone in custody—someone who at least seems to be along the lines of who we are looking for."

"And there's no need to be lazy and flippant about it either," Ava said. "We have no evidence, and the way he talked about not hurting women last night— he seems more worried about maybe spilling the beans on his friend than the fact that he's a murder suspect."

"Listen to me, Gold. It all lines up perfectly *and* we get a known crime boss as an arrest. This is an absolute win for everyone—yourself included."

"But we got the wrong guy."

Exasperated, Frank lowered his voice even further and said, "If you insist on beating this dead horse, I'll give you one more day to do whatever magic you think you can pull off. Two days at the absolute max. And that's not me being an ass…that's me knowing without a doubt that if you drag it out, you're going to have Minard after you. He'll steamroll you and you're going to look like a fool in front of the few people in the precinct that aren't already against you or rooting for you to fail. If Minard asks where you are, I'll tell him you're speaking to witnesses. But that's it. One day. But you're wasting your time. Tony Two is our guy and he's in a cell."

There were about a dozen things she wanted to say in response, but she took the high road. It was another instance where the rules of the boxing ring came into play. You could run your mouth all day long and just waste your breath; at the end of the day, results came in the form of your actions.

With that in mind, Ava exited the precinct and once again hit the streets, this time with the rather odd task of proving that a mobster was innocent of murder.

***

Rather than rushing out and hitting up the few people she knew from her days as a singer, Ava spent a bit of time walking the streets. She made her way to the area where the first woman had been killed, right behind the Key Factory. She then oriented herself to where the second woman had been killed. It, too, was not very far away from a club—though it was not one Ava was overly familiar with.

Close to noon, Ava caught what she hoped was a break. She was passing by a bank and barely heard a conversation between a robust-looking man and a much smaller man dressed in a very nice suit.

"…and one of these days, the women of this friggin' city are going to realize that the right to vote didn't make them invincible. Pretty, young girls walking up and down the street without a fear in the world. I mean, they're pretty much asking for trouble. She could have been dead as a doorknob just like them other two if I hadn't shown up."

Ava didn't exactly care for his tone toward women, but what he had to say was certainly along the lines of what she was looking for.

She turned to the man and inserted herself into the conversation. "I'm sorry, sir, but could you repeat what you were just saying?"

He looked at her with something akin to appreciation at first but then she got the same hazed glare most men gave women who seemed to want to be informed of anything other than what they should prepare for dinner.

"Ah hell, I wasn't trying to offend no one," he said sarcastically. "I didn't mean—"

"I'm with the city police Women's Bureau," she said. "I'm looking for any information at all about these so-called hatchet killings. From what I heard, you helped a young lady in need recently?"

"Yeah, I did," he said. She could tell by the way he pushed his chest out and slightly tilted his chin that was he was extremely proud of it, too. "Last night, in fact."

"Would you be willing to tell me what happened?"

"O' course." He took a moment to light a cigar and started puffing on it before he began. "It happened just about six blocks from here, in fact."

"Would you show me where?"

"Ah, lady, I got to get back to work soon." He seemed torn over it, really wanting to play the part of the hero. "But I can give you the address."

"That would be very helpful. First, can you tell me what happened?"

"I was out after a few games of pool with my brother. We were walking home and taking our time about it because we'd both lost some money and it was late. We weren't anxious to stumble in to our wives, you know? Anyway, we're taking our time and we see this pretty little thing running down the street. She was dressed in one of those tight little outfits you see the dames wearing that work in those clubs, you know? She said she was a cigarette girl, but I don't remember which club. Anyway, we thought it was funny at first, seeing her running like that, but then we see the guy coming after her and realize he's chasing her. And he was a fast one, I tell you what. But we yelled at him and scared him off."

"Did you get a good look at him?"

"Nah, it was too damned dark. I'd say he's average sized, though. White, for sure. But that's all."

"And you walked this girl home?"

"Sure did. Me and my brother."

"Where does she live?"

The cigar-smoking man gave her directions, and seemed almost as proud of giving that information as he had been to tell the tale of his heroics. He told them with such pride that Ava had no doubt that he was one hundred percent correct. And though she knew it was a big city and the lead might turn out to be nothing, it did not take her long to find out that the man was, in fact, spot on.

The girl's residence was an apartment just six blocks away, in a part of town that seemed to straddle the line between the wealthy section and the section that struggled a bit more than most. There were only seven apartments in the place, and the man had pointed her to apartment number 4.

Ava knocked and waited. She listened to the sounds of the building as she did so—someone coughing a few doors down, the sound of humming from next door. And then she heard footsteps approaching the door of apartment number 4, soft and shuffling. The door was answered by a pretty blonde woman who looked to be in her early twenties. The cigar-smoking man had described her perfectly. Of course, she was no longer wearing the outfit from her job the night before. She was currently wearing bedclothes and somehow still managed to look breathtaking.

"Yeah?" the woman asked. "Can I help you?"

"I'm with the Women's Bureau of the NYPD," Ava said. "I understand you were nearly attacked last night."

The girl stared at her for a moment, perplexed. "They got a whole women's division?"

"They do. And I'm on a special assignment. What's your name?"

"Theresa Neilson."

"Well, Theresa, were you aware that there have been two murders in the last few days, and that both were women?"

"Not until last night when those two men rescued me. They told me all about it—told me I was a daft broad to be walking the streets alone."

"I don't know that I'd use that wording, but they were mostly right, you know."

"So what is it you need?"

"As much information as you can provide about last night."

"Sure. Come on in. I've got coffee on if you want some."

Ava stepped inside and looked around. The apartment was sparse, but neatly decorated. It did not have the look of a place lived in by a young single woman. "You live here alone?" Ava asked.

"No. It's me and my mother. But she left for work a few hours ago."

"Does she know about the altercation last night?"

"God, no, I'd never tell her. She already worries too much as it is. Besides…it was honestly not that big of a deal."

"It might have been if those two men hadn't come along."

"Maybe. So what do you need to know?"

Ava thought the woman was trying a little too hard to convince herself that the moment had not bothered her. She was playing it far too cool. "First of all, why did you not report it?"

"Like I said…my mom. It would have made her have a stroke or something."

"Did you happen to see what this man looked like? If you could provide that information, that would be a huge help."

"I just saw his eyes. They were all wide and crazy. but it was dark, you know? And for the first bit, when he was just waiting for me, he was sort of in the dark."

"Was he standing by an alleyway?"

"Yeah," Theresa said, her eyes widening a bit.

"You saw no hair, no facial features?"

"No, nothing like that. Sorry."

Ava let out a little internal sigh. She supposed it *had* been a bit too much to hope for. Slightly defeated, she asked: "Did you notice anything at all about him that might help to identify him?"

"I don't think so. It was all so fast and—wait, you know what? I noticed that he was sort of talking to himself. Or maybe to someone he thought might be there with him, like he was goofy or off his rocker or something."

"Any idea what he was saying?"

"Not really. I heard the word *mother* a few times, like maybe he was talking to his mom." Theresa visibly shuddered here and let out a strained giggle. "It was pretty creepy, now that I think about it."

Ava found it an odd bit of information but tucked it away all the same. A man creeping around in the shadows muttering quietly about his mother…maybe there was something there. She also thought about the figure lurching about at the entrances of alleyways. And while there were indeed a lot of alleys in New York, the fool might be unintentionally making it much easier for her to search the right ones.

First, though, she was going to have to put in some work. Leaving the apartment Theresa shared with her mother, Ava thought it might be time to go knock on some doors.

CHAPTER NINETEEN

It took a fair bit of walking, but Ava returned to the scene of Annie Tate's murder with the first true spark of promise in the case. Annie had died between a clothing store and an apartment building that looked quite like the one Theresa lived in; it was not glamorous or well-to-do but it was far from a slop joint. She was aware that the dicks covering the murder had questioned the neighbors, but they'd not had the new bit of information she now had at her disposal. So, risking the chance that she might be retreading ground that male officers had already covered, she went inside.

This apartment building contained twenty apartments, covering three floors. By the time she'd knocked on the last one, all she'd gotten were cross looks, irritated women, and two men who laughed at the idea of a woman being involved in a serious police investigation. The few people who were cooperative had little to say other than how the city was going to hell or that they hadn't seen anything suspicious or out of the ordinary.

With close to an hour wasted, Ava headed back out to the stoop. There was a lone man smoking a cigarette on the stoop and two children over to the right in the shade of the building, playing jacks. She walked over to the alley and peered in. It looked like about a hundred other alleys in New York—grimy and thin, almost as if they were inviting seedy acts to be carried out there.

"You a cop or something?" a voice called from behind her.

Ava turned and saw the smoking man she'd passed by on the stoop. He looked a little disheveled and dirty but he greeted her with a smile when she saw him.

"How can you tell?" she asked.

"I heard you knocking on doors inside," he said. "Plus…don't the lady officers where those whistles?" he asked, pointing toward hers.

"Guilty," she said, tapping the whistle. "Do you live here?"

"My girlfriend does," he said. "And she won't let me smoke in her apartment."

"Perhaps I just spoke to her, then?"

"Nope, she works as a seamstress at one of them glad rags places. And I work out on the docks, which means I got half the day to fart around and do nothing while I wait for her to ger home."

Ava walked closer to the stoop, figuring she should take any shots that came her way. "Did you hear about the murder that happened here a few nights ago?"

"Sure did. Damn near saw the thing, too."

"You almost saw the murder?"

"Yeah. Missed it by about a handful of seconds, I think."

"Can you explain what you mean?"

He took a drag from his cigarette and thought hard about it, trying to recall the moments. "I was out here, doing this very same thing. Smoking. And I notice this fella walk by, sort of in a hurry. And the reason he stands out to me is because he gave me the willies. He was sort of muttering to himself, you know? It was enough of a clue for me to go on inside, to get off the street. So I stand up to do just that, grinding out my smoke. But then these two pretty ladies walk by. Sort of chittering like younger dames do. I might have even said hello to them…I don't quite remember. I watched them go for a bit," he said, a bit ashamed "You know, sort of looking at 'em from behind. And then I went inside."

"Do you know if one of the woman was for sure Annie Tate, the woman that was murdered?"

"Can't know for sure. I never saw a picture of the dead woman afterwards. But no, I did not know either of the girls that walked by."

"Did you get a look at the man walking ahead of them?"

"No. He was walking with his shoulders hunched and he blazed by, walking real fast. I think he might have had brown hair but I'm not even sure of that."

"You said he was muttering something. Did you hear any specific words?"

"I'm pretty sure I heard him say something like *'Be quiet.'* And maybe something about his momma."

"But you aren't *sure*?"

He thought about it for a moment longer and then nodded. "I couldn't swear to it, but I'm pretty certain he said something about his mother or momma, or mom…something along those lines."

"Thank you," she said, already heading away.

"Sure thing," the man called from behind her. But Ava barely heard him. She finally had a link, though it might turn out to be nothing.

Still, she weighed the meaning of it as she hurried back to the precinct. She thought of going straight to Minard with it—that's how excited she was to finally have something to work with. But she knew Minard would laugh her away and likely remove her from the case altogether if she came to something so weak. She then thought of Frank, but even as she thought of him, a better idea came to her. And when it stuck in her mind, she smiled and put more speed in her step.

She was so consumed with trying to sort the small pieces to the puzzle that she wasn't even aware she'd come back to the precinct until she was starting up the steps. Inside, she barely even glanced at the bullpen. She headed straight downstairs and was happy to see Lottie perched at her desk. She was not surprised to see that Frances was absent; she was likely on patrol somewhere.

"Well, well," Lottie said. "You *do* remember us poor old broads down in the WB!"

"I do," Ava said, sidling up to Lottie's desk. When she looked at the four other women in the room, she wished she'd done a better job of remembering names. Outside of Frances and Lottie, things got a little blurry. As she scanned the other four women, she spotted exactly what she needed on one of the women's desk.

"I'm so sorry," she said to the woman. "What's your name?"

"Deidre Idelman." Deidre was mostly petite, an appearance slightly thrown off by her large shoulders and strong-looking chin.

"Can I see that map?" she asked, pointing to the folded paper on the edge of her desk.

Deidre handed it over and Ava opened it on Lottie's desk. "Anyone know where Frances might be?" she asked.

"Probably her usual beat," Lottie said. "Why? You got something for us?"

"I think I do," she said with a smile. She grabbed a pencil from Lottie's desk and drew a large circle around the area the two murders and Theresa's close call had occurred. "We've got a killer who is using these alleyways to hunt his victims—victims that are all women."

"Yeah…we know that," Deidre said.

"Anything new?" Lottie asked playfully.

"Yes. I believe we're going to find our killer if we stick to these areas and stay on the lookout for a man who is studying women. Also, he seems to be talking to himself. Particularly about his mother."

"My God, men and their mothers," Lottie said with a laugh. "Does it ever end?"

Ava got the joke, but did not laugh. "Not for this guy," she said. "Now, who wants to head out to find Frances to pass this on?"

"You don't want that duty?" Lottie asked.

"I'd like to but...well, I need to go make a personal stop first. There's a favor I need to ask someone."

What she thought, but did not say, was that it might also be time to finally come clean with her father—to let him know exactly how deep things had gotten at work.

CHAPTER TWENTY

Her father's boxing gym was busier than it usually was nearing the end of the day. Two lightweights were going at it in the center ring, and a larger man was getting in reps with one of her father's part-time trainers in a ring off to the side. The staccato sounds coming off the speed bags in the back had a pleasant timing to it, almost like a faster jazz tune as the drummer brought the groove home.

She found her father in the front of the gym, showing a rookie proper footing for a defensive stance. When Roosevelt spotted his daughter, his face lit up like always. It was one of the many things Ava treasured about him; he showed just as much delight in seeing her now as he had when she'd been a three-year-old running for a hug. It had always been this way, even though they saw one another nearly every day. Roosevelt excused himself from his student and came over to her as she half-heartedly watched the men sparring in the center ring.

"You end your day early?" he asked as he joined her.

"Not really. It looks like it's going to be another long day." She knew what she needed to tell him, but it was much harder than she expected. When the words came out, it almost felt like she was delivering bad news. "Dad…in fact, I've been placed on a murder investigation."

He smiled at first, and she knew why. He thought she was joking. After all, women cops simply weren't given that level of responsibility. But when he saw that her own expression was unwavering and tinged with a bit of sadness, his smile dropped away.

"A murder investigation?" he said.

"Yes. And I'm well aware that my failure on this case will likely put a very early end to my career as an officer. I have to do well on this, Dad."

Roosevelt sighed and when his eyes met hers again, she saw that there was a very hesitant kind of pride in his eyes—but it was mostly drowned out by fear. "I read about that hatchet killer. Killing women. Is that what they've got you on?"

She could only bring herself to nod.

"Well, I thought they already had the killer…that Tony Two character, right? Some mob big shot?"

"It's not him, Dad."

"Then why are the papers saying it is?"

"Because it shows the public there's at least some sort of movement on the case. But it's not him."

"So why are you telling me this?" he asked. "I think it's a good thing that they're giving a woman this chance but I'm not so happy that it's my daughter."

"They're using me as a publicity stunt and a distraction from the killings themselves. So I have to wrap this. I have to see it through no matter what it takes."

"And what's it going to take?" Roosevelt asked. She could tell that he was getting more and more upset with each exchange so she saw no point in painting a pretty picture for him.

"I need you to watch Jeffrey for a few days. You're still welcome to stay at the apartment. But I have to give this case my full attention for the next few days."

Roosevelt looked toward the ceiling and said, "He's upstairs right now, in my little hole of a place. He's working on his studies, trying really hard because I told him if he did, he could come down and I'd let him hit the speed bags when I locked up. I love that boy, and I will, of course, be more than happy to watch after him. He's a good kid, Ava…"

"I know that. He's one of the reasons I'm doing this."

"You sure about that?"

"What's that supposed to mean?" The question stung. To think her father questioned her motives was a bit too much; it was almost like betrayal.

"I mean no matter how you spin this, it seems like a play at revenge. And I get that. Hell, I respect that. But keep it in your head that it was chasing after lunatics that got Clarence killed in the first place."

She wasn't sure what hurt more: her father using Clarence's death against her or the fact that he was absolutely right. Either way, it was too much for her to take in that moment, especially when she knew she currently had a few other WB ladies scanning the streets while she got her affairs in order.

When she walked away from her father, she wasn't sure she'd ever felt such hurt and anger from a single comment that had come from his mouth. And as she walked up the small staircase to her father's small apartment hideaway above the gym to speak with her son, the beat of the speed bags in the back no longer sounded like music, but machine gun fire snapping at her heels.

***

Dusk was settling on the city when she returned to the precinct. As she walked up the stairs, Ava caught sight of Frances and Lottie coming around the corner at the end of the block. She waited for them, noting the look of excitement on Lottie's face.

"Anything?" Ava asked.

"No," Frances said.

"Now, that's not true," Lottie argued. "We found out that there's a hell of a lot of men that can whistle very loud. I also picked up a few slang terms that I'm assuming mean *attractive lady*. If you ask me, looking for one crazy man out of what New York City has to choose from is going to take forever."

"Is Deidre still out there, too?"

"Yes," Frances said. "She has a friend who works at that big diner on Bleaker. She's meeting with them, sort of getting the feelers out there. But listen, Ava…I don't know that Minard is going to be thrilled with you roping in more of the WB on this. What about Wimbly? Won't he help?"

"Frank Wimbly is, like many others, convinced that Tony Two is the killer."

"And what makes you *not* convinced?" Lottie asked.

"Tony Two was legitimately confused over the accusations. Besides, if the rumors about him are true, he only uses his hatcher to maim and injure men that cross the mob. Neither of the dead women, or the woman he tried to accost last night, have connections to the mob that we know of. And the way in which they were killed does not line up with the traits of a man who takes a finger here and there."

"Good enough for me," Lottie said. "But I'm calling it a day. If dames like us put in extra time, Minard is going to catch on to us sooner or later."

Ava agreed but also figured she would pull some of the weight after hours, like the day before. Still, she walked inside the precinct, thinking of Jeffrey. He'd handled the news well, and seemed excited that his mother was part of such a big case. She had, of course, decided not to give him specifics, just that it was a big, important case. He also thought it was going to be quite an adventure for him and his grandfather to spend a few whole days together.

103

Thinking of her father brought up the stinging comment he'd dropped on her. She heard it quite clearly in her head…and maybe that's why it snagged on some other thought.

It was chasing after lunatics that got Clarence killed in the first place.

It was mostly true. But that no longer seemed important. It was one word…one word she'd rarely heard Clarence use. It reminded her of something that she felt might be important. She stood partially frozen in thought just inside the precinct doors as it slowly came together. She recalled Clarence in the living room one night, a grim look on his face as he settled down next to her.

"It's a dangerous world out there," he'd said. *"The lunatic I took in today…I've never seen anything like it…"*

Clarence had been tasked with speaking to that lunatic several times after the initial case, hoping the criminal would reveal something more about his crime and anyone else connected to them. And almost every time Clarence referred to this particular man, he used that same word: *lunatic.*

Deftly and as nonchalant as she could, Ava made her way to the records department and took the file for a man named William Snide. As she carried it out tucked securely beneath her arm and out of sight, she got the feeling her day was far from over.

CHAPTER TWENTY ONE

Ava watched the county jail draw closer from the back seat of the Checker cab. Dusk had not yet worked its way to night just yet, but the place had an ominous feel to it. She looked from the building back down to the files she'd taken from the precinct, describing the murders and exploits of William "Willie" Snide. Having read it during the drive, she felt almost dirty even holding it.

The driver parked the cab in the visitor lot and turned awkwardly to her. He'd seemed chagrined when she explained that she was a member of the WB department of the NYPD. But now that the time for payment had come, he was very agreeable. "That's a buck thirty," he said.

"I need you to wait here," she said. It was really just a precaution on her part. She figured getting a cab to pick her up wouldn't be too difficult, but this end of town appeared deserted and she did not want to be stranded.

"It'll cost you."

"I know." This hurt, as any unexpected expense was going to make her start to worry about the financial situation back home. But she had a job now, and she knew the little bit of savings Clarence had accrued would come to her in the next few weeks. "I'll be back in about half an hour."

The driver didn't seem pleased with this, but he said nothing as she got out of the car. As she reached the front door of the prison, she looked back to ensure the driver had not changed his mind. Seeing that her ride was still there, she walked in with Willie Snide's folder still in her hand. She walked to the check-in desk where she found two men in warden uniforms, smoking cigarettes and laughing about something.

"Help you?" one of them asked, making no attempt at all to hide the fact that he was giving her the once-over.

"My name is Ava Gold, and I'm with the NYPD Women's Division. I need to speak with one of your prisoners."

Both men looked rather amused that the NYPD would send a woman on such an errand. "And which prisoner would that be, sweetie?" the younger of the two men asked.

"William Snide."

This took any look of amusement off their faces. "The hell you say," the older of the two said.

Ava placed the folder she'd taken from the precinct on their desk. "I was given his records as proof of my request. If you like, you're welcome to telephone my supervisor, Captain Minard."

She said this only because they'd do no such thing. She knew a man would not want to appear as if they needed another man's approval on anything—not even when it came from the prison system.

"Have it your way then," the older man said, getting to his feet. "Follow me."

Ava did just that. He led her through the small lobby and then to a wide corridor. Here, he knocked on a door that was partially open and stuck his head in. Ava was not able to see who he spoke to but heard the brief exchange.

"Ring Rafferty," the older man from the desk said. "We got a cop here that needs to speak with Willie Snide."

"What the hell for?" came the gruff reply from inside the office.

"Didn't ask. Didn't want to know."

"All right. Head on back, and I'll ring him. Shut the door, would you?"

The man did as he was asked. When he turned back to Ava, his eyes seemed distant and filled with fear. "How many guards you want in the room?"

"Is that really necessary?" she asked.

The man smiled nervously and, ignoring her question, said: "We'll start with two."

***

She was led into a small room ten minutes later. When she stepped through the door, the man from the front desk took his leave, clearly eager to do so. Inside the room, two guards stood in opposite corners, as still as statues. One was rather large, damn near the size of a tree. The other was of average size and looked very uncomfortable. He kept his hand very close to his service pistol, holstered at his side.

Then her eyes fell on William Snide. He was sitting at a scarred wooden table in the center of the room. His scrawny ankle was clasped to one end of a chain; the other end was affixed to a bar that was bolted into the floor. He looked every bit of his fifty-one years. His skin looked almost *too* white, as if he were very cold all the time. His face, highlighted by a large scar that ran across his forehead, was gaunt and somehow ghoulish. Yet when he smiled at her, she nearly found him handsome in an odd way. His head was shaved and the beard on his chin was about six inches long and badly in need of a trim.

"I just love visitors," Willie said, as if she had joined him on a front porch for a glass of iced tea. "Who might you be?"

"My name is Ava Gold, with the—"

"The New York City Police Department Women's Bureau. Yes, I know. I was informed by these humble guards. Gold…Ava *Gold*." He smiled warmly at her as she slowly took the seat on the opposite side of the table. "Any relation to Clarence Gold?"

"He was my husband."

"Oh! I see. Well, that's nice. He is…wait. *Was* your husband?"

"He died recently."

Willie's frown seemed genuine. He then smiled at her again but this time there was something sinister in it. "Let me guess. Killed while working. And now you figure you can take his place and pick up where he left off…making this deplorable city a safer place. Something like that?"

She ignored him, sensing that he was already trying to get a rise out of her. She regarded him for a moment, finding it hard to believe that the skinny, rather normal-looking man in front of her was capable of everything in the folder that she sat lightly on the table between them.

Three years ago, Willie Snide killed his wife by strangling her. He then cut off her head with a hatchet and put it in a suitcase, which he carried with him into the city, with the intent of dropping it off at the house of his mother-in-law. He was stopped by a policeman who noticed blood coming from the bottom of the suitcase, and the officer caught a hatchet in the neck for his troubles. After that, Willie went on the run. It was a three-day chase wherein Willie ended up killing five more people. He killed one by chewing into the victim's neck. Another he hung up in a shed just outside of Amityville and flayed open like a piece of cattle. That was where he was found, removing organs with great precision, and labeling them. In his testimony, he claimed the murder of his wife had been one of enraged passion—but the act of killing had been much more enjoyable than he'd expected and he figured he'd get a bit more in before he was captured.

"That's my file?" Willie asked.

"It is."

"Can I see it?"

"No. Mr. Snide, I—"

"Willie, please."

"Willie, I'm here because I was hoping you could offer some insights into a current case I'm working on."

His eyes filled with childlike glee and he clasped his hands together on the table. "I have no idea why you'd come looking to me for help, but I'd be more than happy to! What do you need?"

"As we've already discussed, my husband brought you in. He was the one who made the arrest. And some of the things he said you did…he described them as shocking. He never went into detail, so I figured it was something quite grotesque. And then I looked at this today," she said, tapping the folder in front of her. "You say your wife's murder was one of passion—one that revealed to you just how much you enjoyed murder. I need to know what that's like. I need to know how to anticipate when a current killer may strike next and was hoping you could shed some light on the nature of why…of *why* people do it."

Willie laughed heartily at this. It was a sound that sent a chill through Ava. It also angered her a bit.

"Why? Well…if you were out in the woods and a bear crossed your path, you'd be scared, right?"

"Of course," she said, unsure of where this was headed.

"And why would you be scared?"

"Because the bear could possibly attack."

"Right. It probably *would* attack you. And why? Well, because that's what bears do. Same with a snake. Snakes bite because they feel threatened. They are snakes. That's what they do. And humans are no different. At the core, we are no better than a striking snake or a vicious bear. We kill. It's in our nature.

"I don't buy that," Ava argued.

"There's nothing to buy. What about that little skirmish overseas? July 1914 to November 1918. That delightful little war is evidence that we are very good at killing one another. That many of us enjoy it."

"I did not come here for any social or civics lessons," Ava said, getting to her feet. "I'm sorry to have bothered you. This was a mistake."

She took three steps away, hating the way it felt to have her back to Willie. But then his voice stopped her. One word in his dry voice. "Power."

She turned to him and glared. "It's that simple?"

"Yes. At the core of why I killed my wife…it was the need to exert power over her. Only…when I watched the life flee from her eyes, it wasn't enough. I realized I had taken a life. I realized that I had crossed a line and I would never be the same. And God, how I loved that feeling. I needed more. I needed…"

He paused here, as if conflicted. "There were things I attempted to do to her before I cut her head off, but simply couldn't," Willie said. "I can go into detail if you like."

"No need," she said her stomach turning. "Explain the line. Crossing that line."

"I wanted more. There had to be more I could do to her than just taking her life. So I took her head off. And as a final insult, I figured I'd deliver it to her mother. But then that damned copper stopped me. And really, it wasn't even a question. I killed him without a thought. I wanted to *really* lay into him. I had this picture in my head of cutting off his hands but I knew I did not have time."

"Please start making this make sense to me," Ava said, sitting back down across from him.

"Have you ever killed someone, Mrs. Gold?"

"No."

"Then I can't properly explain. All I can say is that I crossed that line and there was no turning back. I'm sure there are some people that kill another human—maybe out of self-defense or in a situation like the one we had overseas a few years back—that hate it. That *loathe* it. They take a life and spend the rest of their own trying to forget it. But I was the opposite. It was a compulsion. It was like a child, discovering a new toy and wanting to play and play and play." He was leaning forward and seemed to realize he was getting too involved in his explanation. He sat back and said: "How many has this murderer taken?"

"Two so far," Ava answered. "A third was attempted but he was stopped."

"Then he will certainly do it again. How is he doing it?"

"A hatchet."

The smile returned to his face and she could practically see him recalling the feel of his own hatchet in his hand.

"Where is he striking them?"

"The head and neck."

Willie nodded as if he understood perfectly. "Yes, then he will do it again. As a matter of fact, if he's doing it with such…with such *enthusiasm*, I can pretty much guarantee you this is not the first time he's killed."

"How do you know?"

He grinned, and she could sense a secret lurking behind it. She resisted that particular rabbit hole and stayed on track.

"I need to be able to predict when and where."

"I don't think that's possible. If he's anything like me…I wanted to do it that entire time. I did not sleep for that entire three days I was on the run. When I wasn't killing, I was thinking of killing. I was dreaming up ways to dismember and maim and—"

"Did you hear voices?" Ava interrupted?

"You know, lots of people asked me that when I was captured and they always seemed disappointed at my answer. No. There were no voices guiding me. I did the things I did because I wanted to. Plain and simple." He smiled once again and there was pure malice in it. "Were you hoping to come in here and find that I was crazy? Is your killer crazy? Is he hearing voices?"

"I don't know," Ava said, sensing the conversation coming to a close. "But he's talking to himself. Something about his mother, from what we gather."

"Maybe he's killed her, too," Willie said. This was followed by a roar of laughter through which he also said, "And what man in his sane mind *hasn't* wanted to kill his mother at some time or another?"

When he started roaring with laughter again, Ava got to her feet. "Thank you for your time, Mr. Snide."

"Oh, please don't go! I don't get visitors. People think I'm mad, I suppose." He laughed at this, too; it was as if a faucet had been opened and it was now pouring out.

Ava left the room and found herself in another corridor. But she knew the way to the lobby and her cab beyond. And as she walked toward it, the sound of Willie Snide's maniacal laughter followed her, as if taunting her even now that she was gone—teasing her because her visit to this madman had resulted in the smallest of possibilities.

He'll almost certainly kill again…

And what man hasn't wanted to kill his mother…

Two more pieces of the puzzle, small and undefined, but Ava couldn't help but wonder if there might be something there.

CHAPTER TWENTY TWO

The cab driver seemed to understand that Ava was processing something on the ride back into the city. He kept quiet as Ava stared out to the darkening streets. A very fine sprinkling of rain started to fall and it seemed to fit Ava's train of thoughts perfectly. As she tried to put some very fractured pieces together, she realized that Willie Snide had affected her more than she realized while sitting in front of him. In the back of the cab, Ava felt like she had just left some deep, dark cave, craving sunlight.

With Willie's face in mind, she did her best to recall some of the things she'd heard Clarence say about murderers and psychopaths. He was always willing to share stories of his day with her, careful not to get too grotesque or explicit. Ava had always listened intently, having always had a passing interest in criminal law. Clarence had often described how he and his fellow officers would track killers based on their habits and preferences—on timetables and even comforts.

She used some of Clarence's stories and methods, trying to tie them to what she knew of the hatchet killer. He was using alleys and he seemed to know which ones would lead him to his victims without being seen at very certain times of night. That indicated that he knew the city well. So he had likely been living here for a while. And if he *had* been living here for a while and was killing with such ease, it made her think a bit harder about something Willie Snide had told her:

If he's doing it with such enthusiasm, I can pretty much guarantee you this is not the first time he's killed.

Ava felt like there was something huge there. Watching the drizzling rain from the back of the cab, she wondered how likely this was. And if it wasn't the first time he'd killed…had he been caught before and the police department had somehow not made the connection? No…that seemed pretty unlikely. And if he *had* killed and been caught he would have ended up in a prison just like the one Snide was currently in, and he'd still be there.

But he's been spotted talking to himself, she thought. *And if he has indeed killed before, that combination paints a whole new portrait of our killer…*

"Hey, this is your stop, right, lady?"

The cabbie's voice broke apart her speculations. She looked out the rain-streaked window, not sure how she'd totally missed that they'd arrived back at the precinct. "Yes," she said, faintly. "Thank you."

Ava paid her fare and stepped out into the drizzle. She hurried into the building with the remnants of the last thought in her head. *Maybe he killed and no one knew about it. Or maybe there was speculation. And he's talking to himself…about his mother…*

Ava felt that she was on to something, but refused to get too excited about it. Instead, she walked through the precinct, realizing she had never been inside it at night, other than when she'd brought in Tony Two. Without that sort of commotion, the place was quiet and dimly lit. Oddly, it reminded her of a library.

She started for the stairs that would take her down to the WB offices, but paused at the records department. As discreetly as she could, she entered and returned the file of Willie Snide. She looked at the rows of filing cabinets, wondering if there might be answers or further links to her growing theory. Even if there were, she had no idea where to start.

She nearly left the room, but then hesitated. She went back to the filing cabinet where she'd stored Willie Snide's records and pulled them back out. She read through some of the notes and comments, finally landing on a section she had only glossed over when she'd read through. Early in his trial, Willie had been referred to a specialist at a mental institution, likely trying to determine if he needed to be housed there or in a prison. Ultimately, it had been prison for Willie, but the name and number of the head shrinker who had seen him—along with the name and phone exchange information—was listed.

Committing it to memory, Ava made her way down to the WB office. The room was empty, though there was clutter on Frances's desk. And there was also a candlestick phone. She walked over to it, took Frances's seat, and picked the receiver off of the switch hook. She dialed the four-digit exchange number into the rotary and listened to the hiss and crack as the lines were connected.

After a while, a gruff elderly voice answered: "Rumsfield Mental Facility. How can I assist you?"

"My name is Ava Gold, and I am a member of the NYPD Women's Bureau. I've been assigned to keep tabs on any patients who have been cleared and released over the past year—particularly those who had showed violent tendencies toward women. Who could I speak to in order to get that list of names?"

"That would be Harvey, in records. But he's gone for the day, ma'am."

"Is there no one who can get into the records and give me the list right away?" she asked, pressing.

The man sighed and asked her to hold. A few moments later, he picked the phone back up, showing her that accessing the records had not been very hard at all. "I've got a list here," he said, "but without Harvey, I can't narrow it down to men who only acted violently toward women."

"How long is the list?"

"Twelve names."

"Could I have them, please?"

The elderly man recited the twelve names, and Ava wrote them all down.

"Anything else, ma'am?" he asked, tiredly.

"Yes, actually. There is one more mental institution, correct? Just off to the north of the city?"

"That's correct."

"Could I please have that number?"

The old man sighed, asked her to hold again, and came back moments later. Ava jotted down the number as he recited it and ended the call. She then fired up the line to the asylum just north of the city, expecting similar results. She figured after this, she'd call other local ones: Bellevue, Buffalo State Hospital, Bloomingdale, Rockdale. *Jesus, this is going to take longer than I thought,* she griped to herself.

"Baker Asylum," a woman's cheerful voice said—a stark contrast to the man she'd just spoken with.

Ava went through the same spiel with this woman, starting to feel like one of those parrots at the circus that mimicked their owners.

"Hello. My name is Ava Gold, and I am a member of the NYPD Women's Bureau. I've been assigned to look into any patients who have been cleared and released over the past year, especially ones who showed violent tendencies toward women. Who could I speak to in order to get that list of names?"

Ava was surprised when she came back with only two names. "I've got an Alan Hatfield and Lester Stubbs. But I know for a fact that Lester Stubbs killed himself when he was checked out of here…not even a week after, in fact."

"And what about Hatfield?"

"Haven't heard a thing about him. He was discharged about six months ago from what I see here."

"Any incidents while he was there?"

"None that I know of…other than the occasional screaming fit he'd get into with his mother."

"During visits?" Ava asked, perking up. A little flicker of excitement passed through her; it was almost like a tiny shock of current passing through her.

The woman chuckled nervously. "Oh, no…she was never there. But Lester sure would scream at her as though she was."

"Ma'am, listen," Ava said. "This is very important. I need to speak with someone as soon as possible about Lester Stubbs. He may be a suspect in a case the department is working feverishly to wrap."

"That would be Dr. Huffman," the woman said. "He typically gets in around seven in the morning. Would you like for me to leave a note for him to expect a visit?"

"Yes, that would be great. Thank you."

Ava ended the call with that growing spark of certainty now catching flame into something bigger. She nearly went to Frank's desk to leave him a note, but thought better of it. No sense in getting him involved unless she was *absolutely* sure. Wired with promise and adrenaline, Ava continued making calls. She had just enough of a theory and, in her estimation, a solid lead being built up. As far as she was concerned, nothing was going to get in her way now.

CHAPTER TWENTY THREE

Ava used cash she'd stashed away in an old grease tin to pay the cabbie the following morning, giving him the same instructions. Stay in the parking lot and wait for her to come out. Seeing the ease at which she flashed the dough, the cabbie nodded gratefully.

Baker Asylum was a beautiful building, much smaller and elegant-looking than the institutions in the city proper. The landscaping alone gave it the feel of a hotel rather than a mental asylum. It put her at ease as she entered the front door. And almost right away, that ease was dropped.

She entered through a lobby that looked mostly normal, but as soon as she walked toward the front desk, the comforting façade of the place fell away completely. She could hear someone shrieking somewhere further into the building and there was the faint smell of urine in the air—urine that had clearly been cleaned with some sort of industrial solution but still clung to the air. The walls had recently been painted, though it was clear there was only dull concrete beneath. Even the counter that sat at the back of the lobby looked second-rate. The women behind it, though, seemed to not notice or care about these things.

"Good morning," she said. "Can I help you?"

Before Ava could answer, she heard that shrieking again, lost and far away. It was the sort of high-pitched shriek that made it hard to tell if the shrieker was male or female.

"Yes, I'm Officer Ava Gold," she said. It was a bit surreal, as she wasn't sure she'd ever referred to herself as *officer* yet. "I'm here to speak with Dr. Huffman. A lady I spoke with last night should have left him a note."

The receptionist checked a series of notes on her desk, finally nodding. "Yes, I see it right here. I'm to take you right back to Dr. Huffman," she said, getting to her feet. "This way, please."

Ava followed the receptionist away from the desk and down a hall to the right. Here, just a few steps down, the smell of urine was stronger. She also smelled body odor and some other pungent scent she could not identify. She was led past what she assumed was some sort of common room where several patients were going about their own business. She saw a man of about fifty furiously coloring something on a sheet of paper, and another staring at a picture book, unblinking, with a sliver of drool running down his chin.

When the shrieker further down the hall yelled again, she jumped. Ahead of her, the receptionist only chuckled. "Some of them get a little wild in the morning, as you can see."

Ava had, of course, heard of some of the barbaric treatments that sometimes took place at some asylums. While there were new laws being passed, they were mostly flippant and vague. She knew of the electric shock therapies that, as far as she knew, did next to nothing to improve the state of patients. She'd also heard horror stories about lobotomies, but she would not allow herself to pull those tidbits to mind as she walked through the halls.

They came to the end of the corridor and then took a right. Here, the interior looked in a bit better shape, chiefly because it seemed to be where the doctor's office was located. The receptionist pointed Ava to the second door and then made her way back to the front of the building.

Ava approached the partially open door and knocked while also poking her head inside. "Dr. Huffman?"

The man sitting behind the large desk was slightly overweight and sported a finely combed moustache. He was dressed in what Ava assumed passed as a doctor's smock at this institution, with a set of bifocals tucked into the breast pocket. He looked up to her from a pile of notes and folders, giving her a smile.

"Officer Gold?" he said.

"Yes," she said, noting the tiny bit of humor in his tone when he said the word *Officer.*

"Come on in. I've saved fifteen minutes for you before I have to get out there and make my rounds."

"I appreciate that," she said, taking the single seat that sat on her side of the desk.

"I'm told you needed to speak to me about Lester Stubbs, correct?"

"I do."

"Well, Lester was a—"

He was interrupted by a wailing scream from elsewhere in the building. It was almost like a hooting primate sound. Huffman stood, walked to the door, and closed it with a smile. "Sorry about that," he said.

"It's quite all right," she said, though the entire visit so far had put her on edge. "In terms of Lester, the woman I spoke with last night indicated that he would often get into screaming fits that sounded like conversations with his mother. Does that sound accurate?"

"Yes, that's Lester," he said with an odd sort of joy. It was as if he were speaking about a pet dog he had that was guilty of chasing squirrels.

"What brought Lester into your care?" Ava asked.

"Well, Lester came in a little over five years ago when he beat his sister half to death. He beat her because she refused the gift he had made for her: a dead rabbit, roughly gutted, stuffed with ribbons and bows. He later revealed to me that he had killed three other rabbits, two cats, and a stray dog in an attempt to practice making the gift. We also later came to find out, thanks to the mother, that Lester was also guilty of sneaking into his sister's room at night and pleasuring himself as he watched her sleep. The mother and sister both caught him doing this on multiple occasions."

"Was there any history of him trying to beat his mother?" Ava asked.

"None that the mother told us about. There *were* a few times Lester claimed that his mother abused him. He said one time after he was caught in his sister's room, his mother held a lit match to his genitals."

The imagery was gruesome, but the matter-of-fact way Huffman talked about it was somehow worse. She did her best to seem undaunted and continued. "Did he ever mention wanting to kill her?"

"Quite the opposite," Huffman said. "Lester Stubbs adored his mother. The screaming fits he had usually consisted of him screaming at her for forgiveness. And even when I would try to *make* him say something against his mother, he never did. Instead, he would inflict harm on himself. He bloodied his own nose a few times, knocked a tooth out."

She did not like the manner in which Huffman was telling her these things. Again, it was too jovial—the sort of funny stories he might tell some of his friends on a weekend at the lake.

"And despite all of this, he was allowed to leave?"

"Yes. He started to think with more clarity. He passed all of the cognitive tests and the screaming fits subsided. Whenever there were conversations about his sister, the rabbit, or what he would do in his sister's room, there was true regret and sorrow. He prayed to accept Christ as his Lord and Savior and after that, he was like a new man."

"And when, exactly, was he discharged?"

"It's been about four weeks ago. Maye a bit more."

"And he was here for five years?"

"Yes. Lester came to us when he was eighteen." He hesitated here for the first time and eyed Ava with worried eyes. "I'm sorry…but has Lester had some sort of a relapse?"

"We don't know. We are currently trying to find a suspect for a particular crime and Lester fits some of the details."

"I see. I don't think Lester would…well, he seemed put-together when he left here. I would say I doubt it's him but you can never be too sure about these things."

"Do you know if he and his family always lived around here?" Ava asked.

"Yes. His father died when he was very young, right after he had purchased a place in the city. Once Lester was placed in our care, I believe his mother moved to Boston. His sister married and moved elsewhere, too, though I don't know where. As I'm sure you can understand, we don't really keep up with that sort of thing once they've been discharged."

"I understand that," she said. "But is there any chance at all you have an address for where Lester might be staying?"

"I do," he said. "And I'm fine giving it to you, but I have to suggest that you mention nothing about this conversation. It could easily trigger him and cause him to relapse if someone other than myself approached him about those topics. So if you truly must speak with him and ask questions, keep them simple and veiled."

She nearly said the next comment that passed through her head, but she kept it to herself: *That's a lot of caution—enough caution to make me wonder why the hell he was discharged in the first place.*

"Thank you, Dr. Huffman," she said. "I'll approach him with the utmost care. Now…can I have that address?"

CHAPTER TWENTY FOUR

When the cabbie dropped her off a block away from the address Huffman had given her, she paid and dismissed him. She wasn't too surprised to find that it was a slum. Hell, it was the sort of neighborhood that made a slum look good. There were a few houses, all of which looked to have been slapped together with cheap wood and slabs of concrete. There was litter in the street and a smell in the air that was not too dissimilar from what she had experienced back at Baker Asylum.

She walked the block to the address and found what she was quite sure was a flophouse. She'd heard of them before but had never had the displeasure of actually visiting one. Clarence had told her about them and how gross they were, how fortunate he realized he was after coming back out of them—to have a home and a stable roof over his head.

The building looked like an apartment complex someone had started building and then abandoned near the end. She'd heard the places described as a sort of transient hotel where there were few rooms, even fewer beds, but upwards of a dozen or more men slept in one single room. It made perfect sense that a man fresh out of a mental institution with no family to go to would end up somewhere like this.

As she approached the derelict porch, she spotted a lone man standing against the side of the building. He was relieving himself against the side wall and making absolutely no attempt to hide what he was doing. When she reached the front door, she had no idea if she should just go in unannounced or knock. It seemed like the sort of place where devious deeds went down and she did not want to knock and give anyone any sort of warning. On the other hand, she didn't have Clarence's gun on her so just bursting in without any kind of protection was likely an invitation to get seriously hurt.

In the end, she decided on a mix of both. She knocked on the door, waited a second, and then tried the knob. Not only was the lock not engaged, but the knob felt like it might fall off in her hand. She opened the door a bit and slowly edged her head in.

"Hello?" she said. And after that, the smell of the place hit her. She smelled piss, sweat, hard liquor, and what she could only assume was the smell of countless men passing gas whenever the hell they felt like it. It was atrocious to say the least, all backed by a simmering scent of garbage.

The door opened into a large room with wooden floors, a torn rug, and an assortment of trash. Two men sat on the floor, paying cards. They both looked at her as if someone had just brought them an exquisite meal to eat.

"Looks like our lucky day," the one closest to her said. "Hot damn, sweet thing, you look good enough to eat."

Disgusted and not at all in the mood to be eyed like food, Ava glared at him. "Pretty hard to eat anything when you don't have teeth."

The second man snickered at this while the first man got to his feet. He was wearing clothes that looked like they had not seen suds for weeks. Maybe ever. As he stepped toward her, Ava rolled her eyes.

"Don't bother," she said, showing him her sad little whistle hanging from her neck. "I'm with the NYPD Women's Bureau. You so much as touch me and I'll have half a dozen dicks in here in five minutes."

This stopped the would-be Romeo in his tracks. He peered beyond her shoulder, to the porch and the dead yard behind her.

"Lady, we ain't done nothing," he said.

"I doubt that. But I don't care. I have it on good authority that a man I'm looking to question has been staying here. A man by the name of Lester Stubbs. You know him?"

The man in front of her didn't have to answer. The reaction of the second man, who had remained quiet and timid during the exchange, told her all she needed to know. His eyes went wide and he got to his feet right away. Their card game went skittering across the floor as he went running to the back of the house.

Either this man was Lester Stubbs or he was going to warn Stubbs for some reason.

Ava started rushing forward and noticed right away that the other man—the one who had considered her good enough to eat—was purposefully standing in her way. There was a creepy smile on his face that told her two things: he had no intention of moving and he probably *wanted* her to push him down just to get some action.

Ava elected not to push him. She let out some of her anger in a well-placed right hook that landed squarely in the man's chest as she went running forward. She heard him gasp and saw him start to stumble backward, but did not get to see him fall. She was already halfway across the room and heading down the back hallway in the direction the second man had gone.

All along the hallway, she saw partially opened doors. There were several men in a few of them and she was vaguely aware that they were coming to their doorways to see what was going on as she blasted by. Ahead of her, the suspect took a left and she soon heard a door being opened. Ava kicked her legs into another gear, the whistle beating against her breast as if reminding her it was there. She figured if the man had a decent lead on her when she went out the back door, she would blow on it for assistance. For now, all it would do was rattle off these dingy walls.

She came to the end of the hallway and took the same left. She saw the man just a bit outside of the door, running across the rocky back lot. Ava threw the door open and could see that the man was already slowing, already winded. She did not relent, though. She ran out after him, her feet kicking up dust and her body surging with adrenaline. She was closing in on him quickly, and the man seemed to know it. By the time she had closed the distance and reached out with her right arm, the man had all but stopped. He dropped to his knee and placed his shaking arms in the air.

"Sorry," he said. "Sorry, so sorry."

"What's your name, sir? Are you Lester Stubbs?"

He nodded and looked up at her with sad eyes. "I swear, there are no more bunnies. I thought about it, but I didn't do it…I swear. I've been good, so good. My mother would be proud, I've been so good."

She nearly felt terrible for accosting him in such a way when he clearly wasn't completely mentally sound. She also found herself at a standstill because—whether on purpose or not, she wasn't sure—the precinct had not yet provided her with handcuffs, summonses, and certainly not a revolver yet. All she had was the ridiculous whistle.

"Listen," she said. "I need you to come with me. We have a walk to make, you and I. I need you to walk right in front of me and listen to my directions."

"No. I don't wanna go. I've been good, I swear it. Don't make me…don't make me go back…"

"If you don't listen, I'm going to blow my whistle and male officers are going to come. And they won't be nearly as nice and as understanding as I am. Do you understand that?"

Crying, Lester Stubbs nodded and got to his feet. "I understand. I'll be good."

"Go back to the street and take a left," she said. "You run, and I'll catch you. You try anything stupid, and I'll blow my whistle. Understand?"

Again, he just nodded. And when his back was to her, Ava finally allowed herself to relax. And beyond that, she allowed herself a moment of triumph, feeling certain she'd nabbed the hatchet killer.

***

"Are you out of your ditzy little mind?"

Minard barked this at her from behind his desk, leering at her. He was madder than she had ever seen him and was torn between utter confusion and fear of her job.

"I don't understand," she said. "Lester Stubbs is a better match for the killer than Tony Two ever was. It doesn't seem you're even interested in questioning him."

"Oh, he'll be questioned," Minard said. "That's why I'm wasting an interrogation room on him right now. But at the same time, I'm going to have to figure out a way to make it *not* look absolutely fucking terrible that one of my rookie officers bullied a simpleton! Speaking of which…if it comes up, you need to claim that Stubbs attacked you and that's why you gave chase."

"So you want me to lie?"

"Yes. You lie about it if you have to."

"But I—"

"Shut up. You either do as I say on this or you can kiss this job goodbye." He slammed his fists on his desks to stress the point. But then, as if shifting some mental gear, he stood ramrod straight and sighed.

"Sir, should I—"

"Gold, here's the truly messed up part. Here's the part that makes me want to toss your pretty face out on that street. The move to search in the asylums after finding out this killer has been muttering about his mother…that was brilliant. A good move, even if I do hate to admit it. And I was that thinking that saved your behind on this. Half an hour ago, I was ready to fire you. But…this was a smart move. Just carried out sloppy as hell."

"How, sir?"

He glared at her and some of the anger came back into his eyes. "Because Stubbs was recently out of an asylum, there had to be *very* hard evidence against him for these murders. Let's say he *is* the killer. If you don't find something that absolutely nails him to either one of the victims or the scene, he's going to walk. And to make matters worse, that flophouse you found him in probably has as many as thirty men hunkering down. If even two of them claims Stubbs was at that house the night of the murders, he walks—even if they're lying."

Damn, she thought. She felt like a fool, not having thought about any of this. "I'm…I'm sorry, sir."

"Not only that," he went on. "But being there by yourself while you have a partner was reckless. A stupid rookie mistake. You could have been killed."

"I…I didn't—"

"I don't want to hear sorry, Gold. I want it fixed."

"Yes, sir."

"And another thing," he said with a sneer. "I've gotten two visits from reporters that want to talk with you. Not to mention Frank Wimbly and Frances downstairs singing your praises. Whether you like it or not, eyes are on you. And if they're on you, they're on the entire precinct. Keep that in mind the next time your gut tells you to do something like this."

"Yes, sir."

"Now get out of here. You can question Stubbs if you want, but it'll be with another cop to supervise. But honestly…I wouldn't bother. I already have two dicks out at that flophouse. I fully expect proof of his innocence to come back to me within a few hours. And besides…we still have Tony Two who still could be our killer."

"But what if he's—"

"We just went through this, Gold. Now…*get out of here.* My patience only runs so deep."

She turned and made her exit right away. When she closed the door behind her, she felt exposed. Pretty much every set of eyes was on her as she made her way across the bullpen and to the hallway. Some men were laughing, and very few of them were trying to stay polite about it. A jobbie on the other side of the bullpen stood up and made a dramatic act of stretching as he said: "Hey, Gold, want to race?"

Ava hurried away, feeling her defenses come up, as well as a barbed response. She hurried to the stairs at the end of the hall and retreated to the WB office with the laughter of countless officers pushing at her back. When she opened the door and stepped inside, she saw that most of the women were there. They all looked to her with a mix of expressions on their faces.

Lottie approached her slowly with a sympathetic look and said, "I am far above making jokes at your expense because you ran down a mentally disabled man. And because of that…I should probably not talk to you for the remainder of the day."

She ended this with a mischievous smile as she headed back to her desk. It made Ava feel slightly better but when she looked over to Frances and saw the look of disappointment in her eyes, it hurt Ava more than she expected.

"Do you think Stubbs is really the killer?" Frances asked.

"If you'd asked me ten minutes ago, I'd have said yes."

"But I didn't ask you ten minutes ago. I'm asking you now."

It hurt to say it, but Ava managed to push the words out and it was like spitting out her own teeth. "I just don't know."

CHAPTER TWENTY FIVE

Ava headed upstairs to look for Frank, figuring it would be best to talk over the morning's events with him now rather than later, when the entire precinct knew about it and had enjoyed a good laugh. She did not find him at his desk, and when she inquired about his whereabouts at the front desk with Wayne Gibb, she got no answers there, either. She couldn't help but wonder if he was avoiding her and the precinct altogether, trying to stay away from the drama she had caused this morning. That had made her wonder another thing, something that made her feel guilty, though she hated to admit it: would Minard partially blame Frank for this, seeing as how he was the one who had gone to bat for her?

She was about to leave a note on his desk when she heard her name called from across the bullpen. It was Wayne Gibb, hollering to her from the front desk.

"Gold! There's a call for you!"

Ava wasn't sure how to respond. Should she head down to the WB office have the call directed there? Did she need to find a candlestick phone and have Gibb transfer the call? No one had ever called the precinct looking specifically for her, after all. However, Gibb held his receiver out to her, the cord gently pulling at the cradle sitting on his desk. She hurried over and took it from him.

"Who is it?" she asked.

Gibb said nothing, only smiling. She liked Gibb quite a bit. She recalled that he had been only slightly jarring on the first day but now, unless she was mistaken, it seemed he was something of a supporter.

"Hello, this is Ava Gold," she said into the receiver.

"Ava, it's Hank Armstrong. You remember me?"

She did, and her face lit up. She hadn't seen Hank is years, not since she'd first started to grab shows here and there in the smaller clubs. He was a jazz expert and, the last she heard, was helping to organize concerts for some of the bigger clubs in the city.

"I sure do! But…how did you know to reach me here?"

"Are you kidding? Your name is all over town. There are people whispering that the wife of the late Clarence Gold is hunting down deranged killers. Your name has popped up in the papers a few times, too. Didn't you know?"

She'd been vaguely aware of this, too, but had opted to ignore it. She figured it would never really amount to much of anything. If anything at all, she figured she might be used as a scapegoat if the case went south.

"What can I do for you, Hank?"

"I got a new gig, if you hadn't heard. I'm working down at the jazz radio station. Not the one that sounds like it's being broadcast through a tin can, mind you. The good one! The one that interviewed Duke Wellington a few weeks ago."

"That's amazing, Hank! Sounds like a good fit. But still…I'm a little busy and—"

"Yeah, I know, I know. Listen…I need you on my show. This hatchet killer business is getting crazy, but the news of a woman cop chasing after him is even more exciting. It's a story that writes itself."

"I don't know, Hank. First of all, I don't think there's any way my captain would approve it. Secondly…this isn't about my fame…"

"Of course it's not! It's about keeping the city safe, and about showing how women are just as capable as men in all things! Look, Ava…I've got a slot open at noon today. Two hours from now. I really think you should do it. If you need me to, I can talk to your captain. He'd be a fool to turn down this great, free publicity about how the NYPD is all about equality."

I don't know about the "all about equality" part, she thought. And on the heels of that, there was another thing. She wondered if going on the radio could potentially bring any other witnesses forward. Could she use this as a tool to bring more attention to the Hatchet Killer case without specifically mentioning it?

"The best I can do is ask him," Ava said, surprised to find that Hank's final pitch had worked. "If he okays it, I'll see you at noon. But if he says no, I can't argue it too much. I'm already on thin ice."

"Well, I guess that's all I can ask," Hank said. "Good talking to you, Ava. Hopefully I'll see you soon!"

Ava handed the receiver back to Gibb. As he placed it back on the cradle, he said: "Mind if I throw my twin coppers into the pot?"

"Sure."

"He gave me the gist before I handed the phone to you. Captain Minard will go for it, trust me. He'll pretend like he hates the idea, but he's a smart man. It's great publicity for the department, and he knows it."

This did make her feel significantly better. It allowed her to walk toward Minard's office with something resembling confidence. She was even able to drown out the snickers and crass stares of the male officers as she passed, still teasing her about her morning's blunder. She came to his door, took a deep breath, and knocked.

***

When she entered the station, she could hear Duke Ellington's "Black and Tan Fantasy" being played down the hall. She followed the sound, checked in with a perky receptionist, and found herself being escorted into the recording booth.

Hank Armstrong was there to meet her with open arms. "Didn't I tell you it would work out?" he said proudly.

"You did," she agreed. She looked all around the room, somewhat mystified. To be able to play and listen to jazz music all day *and get paid for it*…well, that would be the bee's knees.

"I know you're busy with the case," Hank said as he sat down behind a long desk filled with strange mechanical boxes, dials, and wires—none of which she understood. "So after this song, we'll get right to it, I've already approved it with the station managers, and they're just as excited as I am."

Ava nodded, looking at the microphones on the desk. When Hank pointed to the other chair at the end of the long desk, she sat in it. Her eyes were still locked on the microphones. Was she really about to do this? Was she really about to turn this adventure into something the public would now be in on? It seemed wrong, in a way. She'd taken the gig in a sort of memorial for Clarence and now she would be speaking to the entire city about it.

"Black and Tan Fantasy" wound down and Hank looked at her, giving her a wink. She watched as he flicked a button and leaned in toward the microphone in front of him.

"All right, New York…that, of course, was 'Black and Tan Fantasy' by the one and only Duke Ellington. And we'll have plenty more just like it in a bit. But for right now, I've got a special treat for all of you. Right now, I have in the studio a truly amazing woman—a woman with a jazz background herself. But for just a moment, we're not going to talk about jazz. Instead, we're going to do some chinning with Mrs. Ava Gold, the newest addition to the New York City Police Department's Women's Bureau. Mrs. Gold, thanks for joining us today!"

127

"Of course," Ava said, carefully speaking into the microphone. She could not remember the last time she'd been so excited and nervous all at once. "It's nice to be here."

"Now, Mrs. Gold…I'm sorry, *Officer* Gold, there are rumors swirling all around this great city of ours that you have been placed on one of the most important cases currently being investigated within the NYPD. Is there any truth to that?"

She knew she'd have to choose her words carefully. This was her opportunity to correct the mistake she'd made with Stubbs this morning—and to prove to Minard that he had made the right decision in allowing this interview.

"That's right, Hank," she finally said. "The Women's Bureau is an integral part of the NYPD, though it doesn't often get much attention. But what the public misses is how the supervisors treat the women of the WB as equals. And by working on this case, I think that shows the NYPD's genuine interest in equality and fair rights for all."

"What about the public? The everyday man-on-the-street? Do they seem to be as interested in this same equality?"

"Not so much," Ava said. "It's hard for some to wrap their heads around the idea that a woman can be just as effective an officer as a man. And honestly, I get it. Change doesn't come overnight. But the NYPD is taking the necessary steps to be the guiding light for it."

"Yeah, it sure sounds like it. Now, as I said earlier, you and I have a bit of a history through some of the city's jazz clubs. You were quite the singer not too long ago…as recently as two years ago, correct?"

"Yes, it's been about that long."

"Any interest in returning to that, or do you see yourself sticking with the WB as a career?"

"Well, that's the beautiful thing about jazz, right?" she said. "It never leaves you. it's always there and it's always speaking. So I don't see why I can't have both."

"Well said, Officer Gold. Now, I'll open the lines up to anyone who wants to ask Officer Gold questions about her job with the WB. It won't last long, because she's got work to get back to, so call now, would ya?" He gave the number a few times and then muted his microphone. Hank gave Ava a nod of appreciation and said: "That was golden! Short and sweet and by God, you kissed the rear end of the NYPD without seeming obvious. Great job!"

The first call came in and Hank took it right away. "You're on with Officer Ava Gold of the NYPD's WB. Say that a couple times fast, huh? Who's on the line, and what's your question?"

A timid-sounding woman spoke up. She sounded slightly older and almost scared to be on the radio. "Officer Gold, I was wondering if you're allowed handcuffs and a gun while on the streets."

"Good question," Ava said, wondering how to spin this one so it didn't look like the NYPD was sending her out unprepared. She decided to give something of a non-answer. "Well, starting the WB is like starting with the plain old NYPD. When you're out on patrol, officers are given cuffs, a standard-issued department pistol, and a ticket book. In the WB, we're also given whistles, and that's what we're told to use most often. This is merely so that the NYPD is better able to protect their women officers while letting the males get involved in the more life-threatening situations."

Hank gave her a thumbs-up as he took the next call. "You're on with Ava Gold! What's your question?"

It was a man this time, and she could hear barbed humor in his voice. "Yes, *Officer* Gold. I was wondering how you have time to raise your children and have dinner ready for your husband if you're out pretending to be a cop?"

"So we'll skip that one right away," Hank said into the microphone. "Let that last caller be an example of how not to act in the face of equality, folks. Next caller, you're on the air. Who are you and what's your qu—"

"I apologize," a man's hurried voice said, "but is there any way to have me not be on the air? I need to speak with Officer Gold right away. It's quite important."

Hank gave her a puzzled look as he said, "Who are you, caller?"

"She visited me this morning and I gave her a name and address. That's all I'll say."

Ava nodded quickly and whispered, "Yes, take it off the air, please." That all-too-familiar jolt of excitement was back and she hoped it actually meant something this time.

Thinking quickly, Hank said, "And hey, folks, we need to go as this gentleman is asking. Seems this is an important matter. But let's thank Officer Ava Gold of the NYPD WB for stopping in and send her off with 'Bell Hoppin' Blues' from Paul Whiteman and his Orchestra."

He flicked a few buttons and nodded to Ava, sliding her the candlestick phone on his desk. "Take it on this. And you're off the air."

"Hello?" Ava asked. "Dr. Huffman?"

"Officer Gold, could you come back to my office?" he asked, sounding urgent. "I have some information you may need."

"Can you just give it to me now?"

"No," he said, the urgency even thicker now "I think it's best we have a face-to-face meeting.

"Of course," she said, already getting to her feet. "Give me half an hour."

She slid the phone back to Hank and did her best to shift mental gears. "Thanks for this opportunity, Hank. Sorry it was cut short."

"Glad to do it! Was that some sort of lead or something?"

"Don't know yet. You never can tell with this job. I'm starting to find it's a little unpredictable."

"Ha!" Hank said, slapping at the desk. "Just like jazz!"

"That's not too far from the truth," Ava said.

CHAPTER TWENTY SIX

Ava thought Huffman seemed different than he had earlier in the morning. He looked more worried and as if the day had beaten the hell out of him even though it was only 1:10 in the afternoon. He also looked irritated. Yet when Ava sat down in the chair she'd occupied just six and a half hours ago, the expression on his face became almost apologetic.

"I'm so sorry to do this to you," he said. "But as it turns out, I did not give you a complete list of possible suspects this morning. This was no fault of my own. There are three other head doctors here, and one of them is currently on a ship headed to Paris for a few weeks. Neither I nor the other lead doctor thought to even consider this other doctor's files because he does not typically deal with cases regarding schizophrenia. I doubt anyone you spoke with on the phone last night would have considered it either. His cases tend to all center around acts of violence—either to the patient's own self or to others."

She almost understood such a slip-up. After all, she'd looked through countless names she'd been given on the phone last night from several hospitals and having only twelve names, they'd all sort of run together as she'd searched the NYPD records.

"But I take it you found something of note in some of his records?" she asked.

"Perhaps," he said. "I would have never even thought of it had I not met with one of my regular patients today. My patient mentioned playing poker for peanuts with another patient—a patient who was discharged a month ago. The name rang a bell, but it was not someone I ever dealt with directly."

"Who is the patient?"

Huffman slid a folder over to her, which she opened right away. A blurry photograph of a man who looked to be in his early thirties stared back at her.

"His name is William Gault. He was admitted a year and a half ago when he admitted to murdering his mother. No one ever took him seriously, though, mainly because of how he described it. He said it was like a dream, like he could barely remember it at all. But he described how he did it, where he did it, and on and on. He even told where the body could be found but it turned out to be a lie. Her body was never found and there was never a shred of evidence connecting him to the disappearance.

"As he stayed here for several months, it became clear that he was likely imagining the whole thing. That, or his mother left him and her imagined death was his way of coping with it. He did seem to have a few mental instabilities and as sad as it sounds, it isn't all that uncommon for single parents to abandon a mentally disabled child at an older age. If that avenue of thinking is indeed true, his adding in that he murdered her gave him a semblance of control over what had happened. Or, at least, that's what we thought."

"And based on all of that…he was discharged last month?" Ava asked, aghast.

"Yes. He was completely rehabilitated and started accepting the fact that his mother was simply missing—that she may have even just left him."

"So why call me at all?" she asked.

"Because I fear his doctor made a mistake in releasing him." He leaned over, flipped a few pages in the folder over, and pointed to a line near the top of the initial interviews William Gault had taken part in when arriving at the asylum.

Ava read it out loud, each word like a little explosion. "He claims to have killed his mother with a hatchet. And then he talked about taking that hatchet out into the streets, out in the midst of a group of women holding a political march. He wanted to kill them, one by one, putting the hatcher right in their faces." She sighed here, closing the folder. "My God. Doctor Huffman, can I see the room he stayed in while he was here?"

"Yes, of course."

They left his office and he led Ava down a well-lit corridor. The smells and noises of the place did not bother her as much anymore. The weight of the revelation Huffman had just handed her seemed to block everything else out completely. After a right turn at the end of the hall, they came to what she supposed was the living quarters for the patients. She heard singing, screaming, and cackling coming from behind several of the doors.

Huffman stopped at the next-to-last door on the right. He opened it up and ushered her inside. The room was quite unremarkable, and had not yet been claimed since William Gault had been discharged. The cot that had served as his bed had been stripped of sheets. There was no window and nothing with sharp edges. Even the cot had its edges sanded down. The room smelled of bleach and stale sweat. Other than that, there was nothing. White walls, plain wooden floors, bland lighting overhead.

To think that someone not in their right mind had lived in this small space—someone who may have killed their mother—was chilling. Hearing the muted sounds elsewhere from the hallway only made it that much worse. She suppressed a shiver as she took a look around.

She walked to the cot and checked it for bloodstains or any sort of hiding spaces but saw nothing. But as she was about to walk away, she did see something…it was small and barely there at all, but it was *there*. On the wall, partially hidden by the part of the cot that held the mattress, something had been carved into the wall. It was not deep and very small, causing Ava to lean over the cot to read it. *Dead hands for dead flowers.*

It had been etched three times, one right over the other. Each line was no more than half an inch tall and the third one in the row could barely be seen at all.

"Dead hands for dead flowers," she said. "Any idea what it might mean?"

"Not right off hand, no. Officer, is there anything else I can do for you?"

"Yes, actually," she said. "I need the last known address of Willian Gault. And I need to use a phone."

They hurried back to his desk, where Huffman searched Gault's folder for last known address. As he jotted it down, Ava used the candlestick phone on Huffman's desk to call the precinct. When Gibb answered, Ava found it hard to believe that she'd been standing in front of him, using *his* phone, less than two hours ago. This was shaping up to be a long day.

Gibb made it less than three words into his answering statement before Ava spoke up. "Gibb, it's Ava Gold. Can you check to see if Frank Wimbly is around?"

"That's easy," Gibb said. "I know for a fact he's not. He was called out on something about half an hour ago.

"Do you know why or where?"

"Sorry, but no. He seemed very secretive about it."

Her first thought was: *What the hell sort of partner is always missing or going off to do his own thing.* Yet, wasn't that pretty much what she was doing? So who was she to judge in such a way?

"Thanks anyway," she said, already hanging up before she had gotten both words out. When she was done, Huffman tore a sheet of paper from one of his notebooks and handed the sheet to her. With William Gault's last known address in hand, she headed back out of the asylum for the second time that day, hoping she wasn't headed for her second mistake of the day as well.

***

Detective Frank Wimbly had seen his fair share of dead bodies during his time as a detective, but the one he was currently looking at made his guts go cold. It was bad enough that he knew the victim, but being that he had also essentially worked with the victim made it so much worse. He hunkered down over the body while two officers behind kept the crowds away.

"How much longer before the friggin' wagon gets here?" Frank called over his shoulder.

"Maybe ten minutes, I'd guess," one of the officers said.

The other officer spoke up, and he sounded terrified. "Might want to put that to the back of your mind," the copper said. "Captain Minard is heading this way."

"Christ," Frank muttered under his breath.

He turned from his crouched position, looking out of the alleyway he was currently in, to the street. There were only a few curious onlookers trying to sneak a peek past the police. As he watched, he saw an intimidating figure approach from the street. Both coppers parted to let him through. It was Minard—and when Captain Minard made a sudden appearance at a crime scene, it usually meant hard times were ahead.

Frank turned back to the body, preferring to see the two hatchet wounds to the face rather than Minard's icy stare.

"Is it true?" Minard said as he approached. And then, as he came up behind Frank, he said: "Shit."

"It's recent, sir," Frank said. "I don't know how someone didn't see him."

"I've got men all over the city right now, looking for anyone that looks to be in a hurry, slinking through the alleys." Minard walked past Frank, then past the body and hunkered down on the other side.

They both looked at the body of Deidre Idelman in revered silence. Her WB whistle hung from her neck at a slant, touching the grimy alley floor.

"Dd you know Ava Gold was giving an interview on the radio when this likely happened?" Minard said.

"Yeah, I guessed at the timeline."

"You know I approved the interview?"

Frank looked up, slightly surprised, but nodded. "It was a good decision. Smart move."

Not taking his eyes away from Deidre, he shook his head. "It doesn't really seem that way now, does it?"

"Sir, there's no way you could have known. None of us."

"Where is she now?" Minard asked.

It was the one question Frank was hoping would not get asked. He hadn't known Ava's whereabouts for almost twelve hours now. He hadn't even known she was going to do that damned interview on the radio until he heard someone at the station talking about it.

"I don't know, sir."

Minard did not respond with the explosion Frank had been expecting. He did look at him with those icy eyes, though. "Did I not tell you to keep an eye on her?"

"Yes, sir. You did. But when she brought in Tony Two like that…I thought it was over. I knew she had doubts, but I had no idea she'd keep digging."

"Seems she was smart to do that," Minard argued. "Because here we are, looking at a third victim, while Tony Two is sitting in a holding cell. Seems Gold was right about it not being Tony Two. It's a shame we'll have to cut her loose next time I see her."

"What?" Frank said. "Why?"

"Because of the timing. Yeah, the thought behind the interview was smart. It's why I approved it even though the thought of it set my teeth on edge. But this murder, occurring when she was on the radio…that's going to be a very bad look. It'll speak of publicity over safety."

"But sir, that makes no sense."

"You saying I'm making a mistake?"

"I'm saying you're *about to* make a mistake. Like her or not, she's good at this. It seems like she's been doing it for years already. Not only that…but if you fire her now after we've already started making a big deal over her, that's going to be some terrible press."

"We have to stop thinking so damned much about press."

"With all due respect," Frank said, "have fun explaining that to yourself when you need votes to keep your job, sir."

Minard scowled at him. Frank's heart was in his chest because he had never dared to speak to Captain Minard in such a way.

"Why do you even care?" Minard interrupted. "You don't even care enough to keep tabs on her." He got to his feet and motioned for someone at the back of the alley to come forward. Frank hoped it was forensics. "Now," Minard said. "Let forensics do their job. In the meantime, I think you and I can go together to let Frances Knight know that one of her ladies was killed in the line of duty."

Frank's heart tumbled at the thought. And behind it was the burdensome news that Ava Gold's job was likely gone. He looked down to Deidre as forensics stepped in, assuming that it could not have been a mistake. To so blatantly kill a member of the police force—and a woman at that—spoke of something far beyond malicious intent.

It made him wonder if the killer somehow knew Ava Gold was the officer actively after him.

And if that *was* the case, then Ava was in terrible danger.

CHAPTER TWENTY SEVEN

For the second time that day, Ava found herself walking into a lower-class neighborhood. There were no flophouses in this part of town, but several houses that looked on the brink of collapse. They were small houses, some of them little more than sizable shacks. What alarmed her most of all was that this level of deterioration was less than a mile and a half away from the bustling part of town she called home.

She approached the house marked by the address Dr. Huffman had given her. Ava's assumption was that the mother had likely been killed in this house—and if that was the case, there was a good chance William Gault may have returned here. Maybe for nostalgia or a feeling of safety and security. From the outside, the place looked vacant, but that was true of most of the houses on this block and from where she stood, she saw a few people milling about on a porch a few houses further ahead.

As she walked to the porch, she again wished she had Clarence's Smith and Wesson Model 10. She'd left it at home mainly because she felt more exposed during the daylight hours. Plus, she had no idea how Minard would act if she was on the clock, roaming the streets with a gun that had not been issued to her by the NYPD. So, unarmed and quite nervous, Ava knocked on the front door. She heard the sound echoing through the house, like a stone being tossed down a cavern entrance.

After a minute passed and one more knocking attempt, Ava tried the door. She thought it may have been locked, but a bit of force popped it open. The door had swollen with weather and heat, the bottom dragging across the cheap wood floor inside. Within about three seconds, she was certain the place was empty. There was a stagnant smell to the air, and it had the feel of a place that had not seen motion in quite a while.

From the front door, she got a view of a hall that led all the way to the back of the house, ending in a kitchen. Almost immediately to the right, there was a large opening that revealed the living room. An old dusty couch sat against the far wall, and a single chair was to Ava's right, tucked in a corner. And it was there that she saw what she assumed was the remaining evidence of the murder of William Gault's mother. The top of the chair had a dark maroon stain on the back, and there were splatters of blood dried on the walls. Some if it had flaked off, much like rust, over the time the house had been abandoned.

Ava looked around the living room, not quite sure what she was looking for now that she felt the place was empty. The last thing she wanted to do in this situation as appear lazy. If this visit did somehow become crucial to the investigation, she wanted to be able to tell Minard that she had been as thorough as possible. So, to that end, she checked the rest of the house over with a keen eye.

The living room was featureless aside from the blood and scattered mouse droppings here and there. She walked down the hallway and saw nothing other than a dead rat, perhaps the source of the droppings in the living room. She looked over the two bedrooms and though she found nothing, became a bit more unsettled. One of the bedrooms still contained a mattress, bare and sitting on the floor. It was filthy, covered slightly in dust. She wondered if it was William Gault's bedroom…if it was the room he had grown up in, had started nurturing his homicidal traits in.

She left the room and then checked the water closet—a room too small and inefficient to be considered a bathroom. It smelled of mold. The small tub was slightly discolored and countless bugs lay dead in the bottom. Ava backed out of the water closet and checked the kitchen, again finding nothing.

Off of the kitchen, there was a thin door along the back wall, partially opened and giving a glimpse of the dusty back yard. There was another door to the right, likely a closet or cellar entry point. She opened it and found that it revealed wooden stairs that led to the cellar. It was dank and dark but she started down right away in the interest of being thorough. The stairs were short and when her feet touched the bare earth below, there was only about a foot between her head and the beams of the floor overhead. With the door open above, a bit of daylight came down the stairs, barely revealing a dirt floor.

The floor had been dug up here and there in a methodical way. Some of the holes were about a foot and a half deep. Ava assumed this was from the police investigation as they'd searched for the mother's body. All the holes were empty, and one had even scraped the pipes for the indoor plumbing in the water closet. When Ava could verify that there was indeed nothing to see in the cellar, she hurried up the stairs and was delighted to breathe in the stale air of the house.

She started back down the hallway for the front door when she recalled her visit to Gault's now-empty room at the asylum. The words lightly scrawled into the wall, barely there and at first sounding like nothing more than ramblings of a madman: *Dead hands for dead flowers.*

"Flowers," Ava said out loud.

She turned around and headed back for the kitchen. She walked to the back door that led out of the house and into the back yard. As she pushed it open, the smell of the house seemed to follow her. She scanned the back yard, which did not offer a lot. It was about a quarter of an acre, closed off from the next yard over by a dilapidated picket fence. As she scanned the fence, Ava spotted what she at first thought might be nothing more than a pile of discarded wood. As she walked closer to it, though, she saw the slightly discolored dirt beneath it and noticed the odd placement of the wood.

The placement looked off because at some point in the not-too-distant past, it had made a rectangular shape. Ava approached it and saw why: it had been someone's attempt at a small garden or flower bed. She saw brittle shapes here and there that may have once been discarded weeds, vines, or roots. A few dry-rotted stems clung to the dirt in clumps.

Dead hands for dead flowers...

Ava's heart felt as if it were deflating as she kicked the boards away. Some of the old soil spilled away. She picked up one of the sturdier-looking boards and poked at the ground. It was mostly soft and gave way rather easily for a few inches but then the natural dirt of the yard took over.

Don't even think about it, a voice in her head said. *Go get Frank. Go tell Minard.*

But by then, she was already going to her knees and starting to dig with the board. Once she tried prying into the ground, the board splintered and snapped. She turned the board around, working with the other end. She got another few inches into the ground before it snapped again. She did the same with another board, then another. On the third, she was about eight inches down when she struck something soft and yielding—something that was definitely not dirt.

She worked around the area, exposing an area of about six inches by six inches. She was sweating profusely by this point, but barely noticed. She found herself looking at some sort of fabric, something that had once been blue but was now a faded gray. She then dug to the right, no longer going for depth.

When the dirt started coming away easier, broken apart by what was buried there, she used her hands.

After about three minutes of using her hands, she jumped back, her stomach riding a tumultuous trail toward her throat.

A face. There was part of a face looking up at her. It was decomposed and ghoulish, skin and tissue mostly eroded away completely. but beyond that and the empty eye sockets that stared up at her, she saw one other thing that was just too difficult to overlook.

Just above one eye and all the way up to the portion of the head still covered by dirt, there was a long, deep groove—the sort that would easily be made by a hatchet.

CHAPTER TWENTY EIGHT

She was panting for breath and coated in sweat when she arrived at the precinct. At some point during her run back, she had removed her shows to run faster, but she had no clear recollection of doing it. When she ran through the doors and directly to Frank's desk, she was not at all surprised to see it empty. He glared around the bullpen and saw that several people were looking at her. The good humor they usually scoffed at her with was not gone, though. Maybe because she looked like a mess, covered in sweat, her hands and arms covered in dirt up to the elbow.

Through the glares, she caught sight of Frank. He had noticed her, standing with three officers and apparently broken from an intense conversation when she'd come in. He said something to one of the officers and then hurried over to her. She hated that every single set of eyes was on them. It made her feel like she was on display…or that they were waiting for some sort of show to entertain them.

When he approached her, Frank did not stop. He took her by the arm, said, "Come on," and ushered her toward Minard's office. Ava was vaguely aware of other officers murmuring all around her but was too focused on Frank's odd behavior to pay much attention to it. In a whirlwind of motion, Frank opened the door to Minard's office without even knocking. He did not *push* her inside, but it was close.

"What the hell?" she said.

Minard sat behind the desk, a mask of worry covering his face. He regarded Ava for a moment, puzzled by her dirty appearance. "I might ask you the same thing," he said. "What the hell, indeed."

"I have the killer," she said. "I have a name and a—"

"Well, we have another body," Frank said.

"What?"

"He's right," Minard said. "Just three hours ago." He took a deep breath and, through a scowl, added: "It was Deidre Idelman."

It simply didn't register for her. Deidre Idelman was a cop. How was she dead? How was she a victim of the hatchet killer?

"Deidre? You're…you're sure?"

"I knelt right next to the body," Frank said softly. "And it was the killer, no doubt about it."

"I don't understand. I don't…"

I sent them out to find him, she thought. *Deidre was out there looking for the killer. This is my fault. I sent her to her death…*

"Gold," Minard snapped. "Do you understand what we're telling you?"

She nodded distantly. "Frances…does she know?"

"Yes. She's downstairs with the other women. We've asked them to take the next few days off until this is wrapped."

"I know who it is," she said. "The killer, I know—"

"Like you knew it was Tony Two at first and made a whole scene about it?" Minard said. "Like you knew it was Lester Stubbs?"

"Sir, you haven't even let me question Stubbs."

"Because I've had other officers that aren't busy making a public spectacle do it instead. And so far…yeah, it seems like you got it wrong with him." He was nearly growling at this point, but he seemed to realize it. He stopped, took a breath, and looked at her as earnestly as he could. "Gold, I know I gave you permission for that interview. But either as a result of that interview or just out of pure unlucky coincidence, it now looks wretched…wretched timing, an awful overall situation. You are no longer on this case."

She had just started to fully process Deidre being dead when she heard these last words. She wanted to sit down but feared if she did, she may never stand up again. She took a single step closer to Minard's desk and lifted her hands in front of her, almost as if she were pushing an invisible force.

"See this dirt?" she asked, her voice somewhere between fury and overwhelming sadness. "It's from a shallow grave I found out on Neibolt Street."

"Shallow gr—" Minard started. But now, it was Ava's turn to interrupt.

"It was at the old home of a recently cleared asylum patient named William Gault, who was sent to the asylum because he insisted he killed his mother by hacking her in the face with a hatchet. The mother was never found. But she's there, in the back yard…"

The looks of horror and bewilderment on their faces may have given her a bit of satisfaction if it wasn't for the overwhelming wave of guilt riding up in her. And on that wave, there was one single statement roaring like an ocean in her head: *You sent her out. It's your fault she's dead.*

"Where did you get the information leading you there?" Minard snapped.

"I looked into local mental institutions for men who had recently been released. I spoke to a…a doctor…Dr. Huffm…"

The world started to sway and she finally did allow herself to sit down. She half-sat-half-collapsed into the chair in front of Minard's desk. She felt her face crumpling up in anguish and felt a tight knot forming in her chest—a knot that would certainly result in guilt-ridden weeping when it broke.

"Ava?" Frank said. "Ava, are you okay?"

"I sent her," Ava said. "I told them my theory and told them where to look and now she's dead."

"We know you suggested it," Frank said. "We spoke with Lottie just after it happened and…Ava, no one blames you."

It did no good. They were just empty words, though somewhere in the back of her tormented head, she recognized that Frank Wimbly was trying to comfort her…in front of Minard no less.

"Go home, Gold," Minard said. He did not sound angry, and it was clear that he was trying to be understanding of her situation. "I told the same of the rest of the Women's Bureau. Go home. I'll call you in after this all blows over and we'll see if we can salvage the future for you. Maybe another precinct, maybe—"

This time, it was Frank who interrupted and even in her saddened stupor, Ava could tell that Minard was beyond annoyed.

"I agree, she should not be here right now," Frank said. "But for right now, I'd like the details of what she found."

"We can't keep chasing her leads, based on how the last two ended up," Minard argued.

"Fine. But she's reported a shallow grave with a body. Even if it's not related to this case, it needs to be investigated."

Minard slammed a hand on his desk. He was getting red in the face, clearly torn in several directions. He leered at both of them before finally, through clenched teeth, asked: "What's the address, Gold?"

"One-eighty-six Neibolt."

"Since you're so damned hot to trot on it, Wimbly, you get out there and see it. As for you, Gold…you can use my office to collect yourself. Then wash up in the locker room and head home. If I see you back here or anywhere near this case, we're not talking a transfer in the future; we're talking about the loss of a job."

"But I discovered the grave, sir. I should go with him."

"Do you not think Detective Wimbly is smart enough to find a mound of dirt you went digging through this morning?"

"That's not what I'm saying."

"Go home, Gold. I'm not going to tell you again."

With that, Minard stormed out of the office, slamming the door behind him. Frank looked down at her with a grim expression. "I have to ask…are you sure about this one?"

"Yes. There were holes in the cellar floor where police looked for the body. But she's in the back…where a flower garden used to be."

"William Gault, right? I'll pull his records. You think he's the killer?"

"If he's not it's an enormous coincidence," she said dryly. Already, though, her thoughts were turning back to Deidre Idelman, the guilt still sinking in like hooks. She looked to her dirty hands as Frank left the office and could only hope the speed she noted in his step meant that somehow, he was still willing to take her seriously.

CHAPTER TWENTY NINE

When she washed the grime and sweat away in the locker room, she felt as if she'd washed the day itself away, too. Somehow, it had become four in the afternoon. When she left the precinct under the scrutinizing eyes of just about everyone in the bullpen and lobby, she could not quite recall where the time had gone. How long had she been digging behind that house? How long had she wept in the shower while the dirt of a shallow grave washed down the drain?

When she came to her father's gym, she was surprised to find the door locked. She peered through the windows and found the place totally empty. She could not recall her father ever closing up early, and he was usually there until six most nights—or even as late as seven or eight if he had a promising pupil in training.

Curious and slightly worried, she walked the six blocks to her apartment building. When she opened the door, she saw her father at the sink, washing dishes. She was pretty sure it was the first time she'd ever seen him wash a dish. He turned to her, surprised.

"You're home early," he said.

"Same to you," she offered. "Where's Jeffrey?"

"You know, I think I might have worn him out today. I let him have some fun with the punching bags. He was at it for *hours.* So he's napping."

"Jeffrey's taking a *nap?*" she asked.

"He is. Wonders never cease."

"Why'd you close early?" she asked, sitting down at the kitchen table. She felt drained, weary. More than that, a sharp and unforgiving guilt was starting to eat her from the inside. While Frank had done his best to assure her that Deidre's death was not her fault, she could not be convinced otherwise. It was almost like she'd sent her directly to the killer—or at least that's how she was starting to feel. Christ, she was lucky Minard hadn't just fired her right away.

She looked over to her father and knew she needed to tell him everything, but it was going to be so hard. He'd worry, naturally, and she feared that same old conversation would arise—how she really had no business in this line of work.

"No one was coming and the only lesson I had this evening came by around lunch and cancelled on me. So after Jeffrey came in from after school and ran hell on the punching bags, we came home. We've only been here for about half an hour or so and—" He stopped here, sitting down to the table and looking across at his daughter. "Ava…what is it? What's wrong?"

She was nearly in tears when she said: "Did you have the radio on at all today?"

"Nah. It's too distracting at the gym. Why?"

"I was interviewed by Hank Armstrong, an old jazz friend of mine."

"You were on the radio?" Roosevelt asked, shocked.

"I was. You know, I always wanted to be heard singing on the radio. But instead, I was interviewed about being a member of the Women's Bureau." She eyed him cautiously and added: "For being at the center of a high-profile case?"

"The same one you had to leave for the other night?"

She nodded, and the tears came freely. Through them she told him everything, starting with Frank Wimbly's suggestion that she be put on the hatchet killer case for a form of publicity and distraction. She went through the arrest of Tony Two and that's when her father started interrupting.

"Hold on," he said. "You're taking down monsters?"

"Yeah," she said, realizing just how foolish it sounded.

"I don't know if I should be terrified for your safety or impressed."

She gave him a weak smile and said, "I suppose it can be both, right?"

With the story coming a bit easier now, she continued on, telling him about how she had chased down Lester Stubbs, as well as the aftermath of the Stubbs arrest. She ended with finding the shallow grave and then learning about Deidre's death. By then, she felt as if a priest had come by and exorcised her. She watched her father's face shift through about a million different emotions but at the end, when she was out of words and her face was soaked with tears, he reached out and took her hand.

"You know I was up for a title shot at one point, right?" he said.

The comment was so unexpected that Ava wondered if she'd heard him correctly. "What?"

"I got a title shot one time. One of the best moments of my life."

As he sat back in his chair, Ava figured he had a point. For most of her life, she'd listened to him spout boxing analogies—most of which eventually helped significantly. So she sat there, emotionally exhausted, and listened.

"The problem is, I got it because I was getting victories left and right and people were starting to know my name. The champ at the time had beaten every lug in the circuit and wanted someone new. So when the promoter came calling with the opportunity and a hefty payday, I took it. But I was too young, too inexperienced, too cocky. I put up a good fight, but ultimately went down in the sixth round. I was never the same after that, of course. I stuck it out for another two years but, as you know, ended up calling it quits after smashing my hand. I still miss the thrill of stepping in that ring to trade blows with another joe. But I love the life I have now…you, Jeffrey, and the gym." He smiled and nodded, finishing with: "Yeah, I'd say it all turned out pretty great."

She did not ask for an explanation. She knew what he was trying to say. He was telling her that she had stepped into the pressure of it all far too soon—only a few days into the job, in fact. It was too much, and she had set herself up to fail.

She wasn't angry with his approach. After all, he was right. Not only that, but she also knew that it came from a place of love and support.

"You okay?" he asked, still holding her hand.

She saw the deteriorated corpse in her mind, peeking up to her from the shallow grave. She saw Deidre's face, her thin smile and strong jaw. No. No, she was not okay. But she couldn't tell her father.

"I'll be fine," she said. "I think a nap with Jeffrey might be just the ticket."

He smiled, as if he understood completely. Ava left the kitchen and made her way back to Jeffrey's room. His back was turned to her and she watched his back move with his breathing. She nestled down beside him slowly, not wanting to wake him up. And as she rested her arm over him, it both broke her heart and angered her that all she could think about was the killer.

He'd made her job miserable and now, somehow, he'd even invaded her thoughts at home. She saw the dark alleyways knitted together behind her closed lids and saw shadows moving through them. She saw—

"Mom?"

She opened her eyes. Her vision was blurry and when she moved her head, there was a light ache in her neck. Somehow, she'd fallen asleep. Jeffrey was sitting on the edge of the bed, his hair messy from the nap.

"Hey, kiddo. Grandpa tells me you're magic on those bags."

"Yeah, it was fun," he said, making a fist. "He says my jab is weak but my hook is lethal."

"I'm sure it is," she said. "Your grandpa has a pretty mean hook, too."

"Why were you napping?" Jeffrey asked. "Was it a bad day at work?"

"It was a little rough, yeah," she said. She was alarmed at just how eager she was to cry in that moment; she felt it behind the wall she'd built up, surging and pushing like a stubborn tidal force.

But even with Jeffrey there in front of her, she still saw the alleys in her mind, a network of secret places for the killer to roam and hunt. And having it creep in while she sat with Jeffrey in his room, she felt like her life was being invaded. She knew in that moment that she was never going to be able to get on with her life—with or without a position within the Women's Bureau—if this case wasn't solved. She did not want to pursue this job if she did not legitimately think she could efficiently do her part to make this world a safer place for her son. She would not let the same sort of world that had taken her husband constantly be a threat to Jeffrey.

She could not give up on this. But at the same time, she could also not disobey Minard.

A knock at Jeffrey's door startled her. Her father poked his head in and shook his head. "Bunch of lazy bums, sleeping the day away. Come on, now, I've attempted to make dinner while you pansies were sleeping."

Jeffrey was up and running after Roosevelt right away. Ava got up from the bed and followed after them and for a disorienting moment, she saw a dark alleyway ahead of her rather than her son's bedroom doorway. She stood motionless for a moment, realizing that she had to go on. Somehow, she had to remain on this case and find the killer or it would haunt her forever.

***

Ava waited until her father was asleep before she headed out. Taking his snores as an indicator, Ava checked on Jeffrey, kissing him on the head. She then left the apartment and headed out to the streets. She was well aware of how dangerous it was—how absolutely risky it was—but she could not stay in her apartment while her mind was on the killer. Her hope was that the streets at night would spur something, would help her to make connections the safety and love of her apartment might hinder.

She did not have Clarence's Model 10 because when she even considered the notion of bringing it, it felt like an invitation to danger. She did still have her whistle, which she'd instinctively worn out of the precinct after her shower. She felt it against her chest as she walked down the familiar streets. When she came to alleyways, she peered down them as if expecting the killer to be there, waiting for her.

She had no destination in mind, just relying on the streets and the night to speak to her. She recalled how Clarence would often take walks at night just to clear his head, to get a feel for the shape, size, and breadth of the growing city. She ran the current milestones of the hatchet killer case through her head, hoping to make sense of it all— hoping that at some point during the afternoon Frank had indeed headed out to Neibolt Street to properly inspect the shallow grave. She went through the chain of events that she would take if they knew without a doubt that William Gault was the killer. She wondered what steps would be taken after the grave was properly investigated after Gault's records were passed around the precinct.

She halted her thoughts when she realized she had ended up nearing the construction site of the Chrysler Building. The progress being made was quite spectacular, even to the casual passerby. The ingenuity and progress present in the nearly twenty-five stories that had already been framed was incredible. It made her ache for Clarence, who had always been fascinated with construction sites. Once, when she asked him why construction appealed to him, he'd answered with a simple statement that had always stuck with her: *Because human beings are simple creatures and the construction of large buildings is proof that despite our simplicity, we have grand ambitions.*

She thought of that comment as she looked at what was to eventually become the Chrysler Building. She also wondered what Clarence might do if he was in the thick of her current situation. How would he evaluate the murderer? What strategies would he use to track the killer down?

Staring at the construction site, she thought about how he had sometimes come home with stories from work—most notably how he often came to a conclusion that helped to break a case. She thought of how Clarence might come up with a way to find the killer and then, in a moment of clarity that nearly dwarfed the construction in front of her, it slowly started coming to her.

She thought of the victims, one by one. Two women who were huge advocates for women's rights. One woman who used her body to enhance her job, getting tips and being a constant object of lust and affection. And then, of course, there was Deidre Idelman—a female cop. They were all women who had a degree of power and influence.

But killing a cop...that was sheer insanity.

Unless he heard the interview, a voice in her head said, and by God it almost sounded like Clarence. *What if he heard the interview yesterday and chose to come after you? But maybe he just couldn't be patient enough...maybe he killed the first woman cop he saw.*

If that was the case, he certainly knew by now that he'd killed the wrong cop. And if he was truly out to kill women in powerful positions...

Ava smiled, gazing up at the struts and girders of the building-in-progress.

A plan started to unfold in her head and when it did, it came quickly. When she turned and walked back toward her apartment building, she had a blueprint that might lure the killer out. And by the time she laid her head back on her pillow half an hour later, she had a full-fledged plan.

CHAPTER THIRTY

"What the hell are you doing here?"

Frank stopped her as she entered the door. Behind him, the precinct was not yet truly alive with the morning buzz. She knew this meant Minard would not be in yet—which had been part of her plan. And now it looked like Frank was going to mess it up. She knew that if Minard came in the doors in the next few minutes and saw her, she'd be done for.

"I just need to get down to the Women's Bureau for a second," she said.

"What for?"

"Frank, please…I can't just let this sit. And…I was sort of hoping you'd come with me."

"With you?" he asked, clearly shocked. "Where?"

"Downstairs. But just for a few minutes. I have a plan. I'm pretty sure I can draw the killer out."

"You know how crazy you sound, right?"

"I do," she admitted. "But I can't just ignore this. I can't just stop it."

Frank looked around the precinct. The bullpen was basically empty, but Ava knew that he was aware it would be a very different story in about half an hour. When he looked back to her, there was worry in his eyes.

"You're obsessed, you know that?" he said.

"No. I just need to get this killer. I have to prove it to—"

"Ava, you have nothing to prove."

"I have to prove it to myself. And if I screw it up, the worse that happens is that Minard fires me. Which it seems he might be ready to do anyway."

"Fine," he said. "Five minutes, Gold. Five minutes and then I'm coming right back up here. And this plan had better be good."

She said nothing else and headed straight for the WB. From what she could tell, no one paid much attention to her as she crossed the building and headed downstairs. She opened the door and, as she expected, only found Frances and Lottie.

"Correct me if I'm wrong," Frances said. "But you're not supposed to be here, are you?"

"That's right," Ava said.

"So is *he* here to arrest you?" Lottie asked, nodding to Frank with sarcasm.

"Frances…I have a plan," Ava said. "And it's going to be so much easier if the three of you can help."

"What sort of plan?" Frances asked.

"To finally get this killer. I know I can do it…I know what he's gunning for. I just need a bit of help."

"And he's helping?" Frances asked, pointing to Frank.

"I don't know yet," Frank said. "I'm still waiting to hear the plan."

All three of them looked to Ava and she started to speak. Even to her own ears it sounded crazy at first but by the time she was done, she felt certain it would work. There was not a single doubt in the world. Not even when Frances made the first comment.

"You're out of your pretty little mind," she said.

It wasn't the first time Ava had heard this statement, but it *was* the first time she'd heard it from a woman. Frances glared at her from across her desk. Ava had expected it, but she wasn't going to be silenced so easily. It was 8:30 in the morning and she understood that her theory and her plan were a bit too much to buy into at such an early hour.

Ava was currently standing in the center of the WB office. Frances was stationed at her desk, and Lottie was standing to the right. They were the only two to come in today on the heels of Deidre's death. Standing just inside the doorway, Frank Wimbly eyed Ava with something very close to distrust. He'd refused to come down here with her at first, citing Minard's orders for her to stay away. She looked at him now, hoping his account might help sway Frances and Lottie.

"Detective Wimbly," she said, "why did you decide to come down here with me? It was evident upstairs that you did not want to."

He rolled his eyes at her, apparently aware of what she was trying to do. Ava knew that he was on to her—he knew she was putting him on the spot in front of these other two female cops. She was using him as validation. "First of all, because Captain Minard isn't here to scream at both of us. Secondly, because I visited the house on Neibolt Street and saw the shallow grave. The body was exhumed, and it was clearly evident that the woman was killed with three sharp blows to the head with a hatchet."

"So do you think I was right to go there?"

"Yes," he said, clearly not wanting to give the answer.

"And do you think the killer targeted Deidre, or do you think he was out looking for me?"

"Looking for you. Gold, what is this? Why are you interrogating me?"

"Because I need all of you to know that I'm on to something here. And forgive me for saying so, but…I could carry my plan out without any of you. I didn't have to come to you. but I did, because it's the smart thing to do. It's safer. Easier."

Lottie spoke up, her arms crossed and her eyes bright. "Darling, the plan is just about the craziest scheme I've ever heard. And that's saying a lot. But I don't have a doubt it will work. Not a bit. Even if he *wasn't* looking for you specifically, I agree with you that he's going after women with power. And with this plan, you'd be damn near the most powerful woman in the city for a day or two."

"Want me to level with you?" Frank asked.

"Probably not," Ava said. "But I guess you should."

"The plan isn't awful. It's risky, though, and I think you're a ditzy broad for even considering it. The one reason I can't get on board with it is because you'd be going against Minard's commands. You're already going against his command because he told you not to show up again after yesterday. And while I'm sure you're a perfectly fine person, I'm not ready to lose my job for you."

"You won't. When it's all over, Minard doesn't need to know you were part of it at all."

Frank looked around the room to Frances and Lottie. He shook his head, whispered a curse, and said: "Go through the plan one more time."

She did. It only took about three minutes this time (compared to the ten minutes it had taken the first time) and by the time she was done, she could tell that she had Lottie and Frances on her side. With the plan discussed a second time, Frank stepped further into the office. He closed the door behind him and looked to the candlestick phone on Frances's desk.

"Fine," he said. "Go on. Call the radio station."

***

Ava walked back into the radio station on Broadway at a few minutes past noon. Just like on her previous visit, Hank Armstrong was ecstatic to see her. Before he led her back to the broadcast booth, they

153

went over the script one last time. Hank seemed pleased to help, but also a little cautious.

"This isn't false advertising, now is it?"

"No, not at all. I've already spoken with Jack Dooley at the Key Factory. He's lining a band up as we speak."

"Hot damn! I might even have to make an appearance then. This is not something I want to miss! You want some air time? Want me to interview you?"

"No, that's okay. Just…with so much on the line, I thought I should be here when it goes on the air."

"Of course," Hank said, clapping his hands. "I'll make the announcement after the current song."

They sat together in the booth and listened to the last half of "Crazy Blues" by Mamie Smith. Ava's nerves were on fire but the level of excitement escalating inside of her mostly drowned it out. When the song reached its end, Hank gave Ava a wink and positioned himself behind the microphone. He started the recorder and then began to speak.

"Ladies and gentlemen, your old buddy Hank does what he can to keep his ear to the streets. I always like to hear about new musicians first and I especially love to play them right here on your favorite station before anyone else. But today…oh boy, I've got something for all of you jazz lovers out there that's going to get you all up in a tizzy! Our good friend Ava Gold, the NYPD Women's Division superstar, has a treat for you all. Seems that when word got out she's a fine singer as well as a fine cop, people got very interested. And for that reason, our friends down at the Key Factory have a special treat for you all tonight. Tonight, for one night only, Mrs. Ava Gold will be performing with a specially assembled band. The show starts at nine, folks…and believe me, you don't want to miss this one! Come on down and have a listen and support this wonderful lady, and your local jazz clubs! That's nine o'clock tonight, Mrs. Ava Gold at the Key Factory!"

He stopped recording, pulled away from the microphone, and set up another song. When it was playing, the drums leading in for a pair of trumpets, Hank looked over to Ava. "That work for you?"

"That was perfect, Hank!"

"Good! I'll play it once every half hour just to make sure words gets out."

"Thanks so much, Hank. If this goes well, you could end up playing a big part of catching a mass murderer."

"That sure would be something," Hank said. "Bust listen: you be careful out there tonight. And most importantly of all, you tell that bum Jack Dooley to save me a table."

CHAPTER THIRTY ONE

When she arrived at the Key Factory, Ava's nerves were surprisingly calm. Maybe it was the stage or the familiar building—or maybe even some of the familiar faces. Even an hour before the show was set to begin, there was a warm familiarity that seemed to seep right into her bones. There was a calm to the place that she always thought of as the quiet before a thunderstorm; you could see the dark clouds rolling in but there was nothing yet—just silence.

She felt it the strongest when she met with the band. She'd not played with any of the artists, but knew of two of them by reputation alone. They talked about the proper set list and what sort of approach to take; they were to perform ten songs, all of which the band knew relatively well, and Ava knew all of the words to. She's been selective with the songs, not wanting anything that would really test the vocal abilities that she had not pushed in over a year. She'd get a few runs and a high note here and there, but noting over the top. Ava's nerves started to act up. She felt a little guilty when she realized they were there mostly because of the gig—not the possibility that the killer might be in the crowd and that her career could very well be on the line.

With the setlist decided on, Ava started to work her way through the crowd. She chatted with a few familiar faces from her past and had to remind herself that, unlike Hank Armstrong, Jack Dooley had no idea that Ava asking to sing at the Key Factory was all part of an elaborate sting operation. If he had known, Ava doubted he would have greeted her with such a vibrant smile. Even an hour before the show was set to start, the Key Factory had filled up to almost its maximum capacity. It had been a while since Ava had been on a stage and she doubted the vast majority of the people in attendance would even recognize her.

With her nerves still all over the place, Ava would have done anything for a nice, stiff drink. She of course knew that Jack could easily arrange that for her, but she didn't think it would be right for a cop to take an illegal drink when the very owner of the place could be arrested for having booze.

As it got closer to showtime, she saw that Hank Armstrong had indeed showed up. He gave her a wink and a *get on with it* gesture. The band was on stage, making their final adjustments, and when the drummer took his seat behind the bass drum and looked at her, she knew there was no more stalling. She walked up on the stage with her heart in her throat.

Even before she started singing, there was a thunderous roar of applause. She looked out and for the first time, realized there were lots of women in the crowd—perhaps there to support her as a cop, a singer, maybe even a mother and widow. She smiled out to them all and raised a hand in greeting. Scanning the crowd, she saw Frances sitting near the back. On the other side of the building, leaning against the wall and fitting in a little better than Ava expected, was Frank.

Seeing them, her nerves settled a bit. So when the drummer led in with the intro to a local piece that had been bouncing around the clubs lately—a vocal-based tune called "Heavy City Rain"—Ava wasn't as terrified as she thought. In fact, when she stepped up to the mic, she was surprisingly at ease.

By the time "Heavy City Rain" was over, half of the crowd was on their feet and dancing. Her voice, not having sung in a few months, cracked a few times, but no one seemed to notice. The band paused for only a moment and then went into a Love Austin song. It wasn't a very popular one, but the crowd did not seem to care. There was loud applause, delightful yelling, and the sound of cheap shoes slamming and tapping on the floor as the crowd danced. Ava sang it with compassion because it had been one of Clarence's favorites. She nearly got choked up and had to keep reminding herself that this was more than just a gig. She was trying to draw out a killer.

As Ava worked her way through the set, she had to hold back tears a few times. God, but she had missed this. Not just the crowds and the singing, but the feeling of music totally capturing a room. She could feel the bass and the drums and each note from the horns pressing against her. She could feel the thrum of it in her body. Her lungs ached when she held the longer notes and it was bliss.

She was sweating by the time the eighth song started—a slower one, giving her voice a bit of a break. She looked the crowd over during this rest and again noted Frances and Frank. They both looked surprised, almost in awe of what she was able to do on the stage. Ava wanted to take some sort of reward from that, but there was another thought that dulled it: *There's a good chance the killer is also out there in this crowd somewhere.*

This thought sat heavy with her until she came to the final song. The band waited behind her, all beaming and coated in sweat. Ava approached the mic and, wiping sweat from her own brow, did her best to play her part while also tipping her hand for the killer if he was in the crowd.

"Thank you all so much for coming out and making me feel welcome. This next tune is the last of the night and—"

This was greeted by groans and boos, which she smiled through.

"—I hope it sends you off well. You see, in addition to my work as a policewoman, I'm also a mother. And I have a special little boy waiting for me back home. So get your feet moving to this one for me, would you?"

With that, she and the band launched into a sped-up, horn-infused version of Gene Austin's "Bye Bye, Blackbird." For Ava, it was over far too fast. After the last note, the crowd applauded her through a haze of sweat and cigarette smoke. She spotted Frank and Frances shifting a bit in the back. As Ava made her exit from the stage, she spotted Frank heading out the door and back onto the street.

As politely as she could, Ava made her way through the crowd as several people tried speaking to her. One of these people was Jack Dooley. He was smiling so wide she thought his face would split in half.

"You *have* to come back," he said. "Did you hear that crowd? They adored you!"

"Well, it's certainly nice to be adored," she said as she walked over to the old bar area. She reached under it and retrieved her purse, which she'd stashed there for safekeeping earlier. "But Jack, I really do need to get going. I'll come by and visit again soon, though, okay?"

"You better!"

Ava slowly made her way out of the crowd, pressed against the wall. After a few more greeting from people in the crowd, she finally made it to the door. There, she saw that Frances had also made her exit. Ava pushed through the door and when she stepped out into the street, the fresh air was welcome. She loved the vibe and energy of a show, but she'd nearly forgotten just how suffocating some of those smaller venues could be when they really packed the house.

Wasting no time, Ava started forward. She was already certain of the route she would take. It was essentially a shortcut back to her apartment, so it wasn't even like she was really going out of the way. It would take her down two alleyways, though, and that was where she felt the killer would approach her.

She came to the first alley and stepped in. The darkness and shadows fell around her like a cloak. Ava took a deep breath and looked inside her purse where Clarence's Smith and Wesson Model 10 gleamed softly. She then cast her eyes ahead and walked further into the darkness.

CHAPTER THIRTY TWO

She hated that every sound she heard scared her. When a feral cat snaked its way between a garbage bin and the wall of the neighboring building, Ava nearly drew her Model 10 out of her purse. When she heard a man's laughter from somewhere on the other side of the alleyway, she was sure it was the killer—William Gault—mocking her from behind for a moment.

She came to a split in the alley after a few moments. Straight ahead would take her into an area she was not familiar with. A left would lead her closer to home and the second alleyway that would take her there. She took the left, not wanting to veer away from her plan. She walked the alley, still feeling the pulse and thrum of the music inside of her. She knew she'd still feel it tomorrow, bouncing in her head like a strange, pleasant headache. She thought about what Jack had said, about *having* to do it again and—

Her train of thought was broken when a man stepped out of the shadows up ahead. He was standing directly between her and the street, his back perhaps twenty feet away from the end of the alley and the street beyond. The light in the alley was almost non-existent but his posture implied that his hand was hidden in a coat of some kind—which was odd in and of itself being that it was almost an eighty-degree night.

Ava kept walking, pretending she had not yet noticed him. When the man started walking forward to meet her, she slowed and eventually stopped.

This is it, Ava thought *This is the killer…be on your guard. Be ready to fight.*

"Are you Ava Gold?" the man asked. His voice was charming, almost sweet.

Ava slowly reached into her purse for the Model 10. The man apparently did not see this. He kept walking closer, closing the distance to less than five feet now.

"I am. What is it to you?"

"Nothing, I just—"

He came at her then, the hand coming out of his coat. Ava pulled the pistol from her purse, only to have the barrel snag on the inside. By the time she freed it, the man had struck her. His shoulder went hard into her chest, spinning her against the building behind her. As her back struck the wall, she raised the Model 10 and fired. She instantly heard the sound of a ricochet, indicating she had somehow missed the man from this close up—likely because when he'd struck her, he'd gone low. For what, she wasn't sure, but she could feel him trying to drag her down to the ground.

The man wasn't especially strong, but there was as urgency to his movements. It almost seemed like he *knew* he didn't have long. Or maybe he had not been expecting the sort of defense she had managed to dish out to this point—and certainly not the presence of gun.

She could not get a good enough angle to reposition the gun, so she settled for a left-handed upper cut. She was not strong at all in her left arm but when her fist clipped the man's chin, there was enough force behind it to make him stumble back. When he fell on his backside, Ava noticed another figure coming down the alleyway. This one was coming from the street. There was just enough light from the streetlamps reaching this figure for her to see that it was Frank Wimbly. Behind him, Frances also came bounding into the alley.

At about the same time the man started to get up from the ground, Frank was there. He shoved the man hard against the wall and pulled out a set of handcuffs with lightning speed. Ava grabbed the man, spun him around, and slammed him back into the wall for Frank to get a better position to cuff him.

"William Gault," Frank said, "you're under arrest for the murders of three women, the attempted murder of a fourth, as well as the murder of your mother."

"Mother?" the man asked, incredulous. "You daffy copper, what the blue hell are you talking about?"

"Save it, Gault," Ava said as Frank spun him back around to face them. "You've been—"

She saw the man's face and her heart sank. "Damn," she said.

"What is it, Gold?" Frank asked.

"Ava?" Frances asked, stepping behind her.

"It's not him," Ava said. "This isn't William Gault."

Frank eyed the man hard and then uttered his own curse. He shoved the man back against the wall again in frustration. "You're right. What the hell is going on?"

"Who the hell is William Gault?" the man asked.

"Who are *you*?" Frank asked.

"Like I'm gonna tell you," the man said. He then spat into Frank's face.

Before Frank could retaliate, Ava did it for him. She went to work on the man's midsection like it was a punching bag. Three quick sharp hooks that doubled him over. She then righted him and delivered a jab to his face that sent him rocking back against the wall yet again.

"Hey!" the man screamed. "You can't do that!"

"You attempted to attack a female officer," she said. "We can do worse if we want."

She drew back her fist to prove her point, but Frances stepped between her and the attacker.

"Hold on," Frances said. "You're both sure this isn't Gault?"

"Positive," Frank said.

"There's a photograph of Gault in his records from the asylum. This looks nothing like him. Which brings us back to the question…" Ava reared back to punch him again. "Who are you?"

The man cowered against the wall, flinching out of fear of the punch. "Little Johnny Jones!"

"Who?" Ava asked.

"Ah, hell," Frank said. Turning to Ava, he said, "Little Johnny Jones. An accomplice of our friend Tony Two. Another mobster. Coming to put a scare into you, I bet. Trying to send a message for takin' in Tony."

"That's right!" Johnny said. "You had no right to—"

Ava acted as if she was going to deliver the punch again, and that shut him up.

"So now what do we do?" Frances asked.

"Well, we're still taking this one in," Frank said, tapping Little Johnny Jones on the shoulder. "Officer Knight, would you walk Little Johnny to the corner and blow on your whistle. I saw another officer—Officer Talbott—just a block or so down on our way over. He'll escort you to the station. I'd like to walk Ava home, just in case."

"Of course," Frances said, giving Little Johnny Jones a polite shrug toward the street. He griped and complained the entire time, but Frances was undeterred.

"You okay?" Frank asked her.

"Physically, yes. But that just means—"

"I know. Our guy is still out there."

"And my plan did nothing."

"But it was a good plan," Frank said. He grinned and said, "It drew the creeps out, just the wrong one."

They heard Frances blowing her whistle from the street and both looked in that direction. "Come on," Frank said. "Let's get you home."

She nodded as they walked down the alley. But just before they reached the sidewalk, Ava looked back. The killer was still out there, and it was far too easy to imagine that he might be somewhere right behind her, peering at her from the shadows he'd already used to take three lives.

CHAPTER THIRTY THREE

William Gault had been at the Key Factory and watched the entire performance. As much as he loathed Ava Gold, he had to admit she was one hell of a canary. Not bad to look at, either. When the show was over and he watched her leave the stage, William dashed for the door, wanting to get out before her. But when he was just a few steps away from the door, his mother spoke up in his head, stopping him.

What are you going to do, just kill her right in front of the place with all these people around? What are you, an idiot? Be patient.

The bitch was right, and he hated when she was right.

He *had* slipped out of the club almost right away but he had not chased after her as he'd wanted. It had smelled like a trap. But it didn't matter. He could wait a bit longer. If she had indeed tried springing a trap, he knew where she'd let her guard down—where she'd start to feel safe.

It would be her home. And as luck would have it, he knew where she lived.

Finding out had been quite easy. After realizing he'd killed the wrong woman officer yesterday, he'd taken some time to really think things over. The one newspaper article he'd read on Ava Gold had not only informed him that her husband had been a police officer, killed in the line of duty, but that her father had once been quite famous. The article claimed that her father was once-great boxing legend Roosevelt Burr. Earlier today, just after he'd heard the announcement on the radio, he'd walked down to Roosevelt's boxing gym. The man had not been there, but some basic questions asked to the trainees and boxers at the gym told him all he needed to know. It had been almost criminally easy. One boxer in particular told him Roosevelt usually just slept in a little loft over the gym, but ever since his daughter's husband had died, he'd been spending a lot of time at her apartment to help with his grandson.

So he'd stayed on that block for the rest of the day. He quickly found out that he'd missed Roosevelt by about ten minutes. He'd taken the grandson out to get some sweets at the candy shop. He watched them enter and then leave an hour and a half later. After that, it had been simple. He followed them to an apartment building six blocks away and waited just to make sure they stayed.

About forty minutes later, Ava Gold herself appeared and went inside.

So upon leaving, with Ava still in the building, William left and headed in the direction of Ava's apartment building. He stood there now, waiting, watching.

It took a bit longer than he expected, but she finally showed up. Only, when she did, there was a man with her. Disappointment rose up in him but when he saw the man had no intention of going inside with her, he was able to calm himself. He ran his fingers along the handle of the hatchet tucked within the band of his pants. He could also feel the blade poking his skin.

He could barely wait.

He was trembling with anticipation by the time the man turned away and headed back down the street.

William watched Ava Gold enter the apartment building. When he saw the man walk across the block and then out of sight, William made his move. He moved slowly across the street. The other man was well out of sight by now, but William did not want to take a chance. He remained slow and steady until he came to the stairs leading up to the doorway to the apartment building. Then he threw caution to the wind and sprinted up the stairs.

He was sure it was just his imagination, but when he passed through the doors and into the hallway, he thought he could hear her footsteps on the stairs ahead of him—he thought he could smell the sweat coming off of her, lingering from her performance at the club.

William made his way to the stairs and kept his ear tuned for the sounds of her movement. He followed her up, a flight or two behind her, and started to withdraw his hatchet.

CHAPTER THIRTY FOUR

As Ava came to her door, she wasn't quite sure which she felt more dejected about: that her plan had netted nothing other than a vengeful mobster, or that she was being moved to something else when she got to the precinct tomorrow. She had been on the job for less than a week and had already managed to become the laughingstock of half of the station and attract the ire of Captain Minard. And once she was taken off of this case or, even worse, transferred to another precinct, she'd never be taken seriously again.

She stopped at the door, considering it all. It was yet another tale of failure she'd have to tell her father. He'd been sacrificing his time at the gym to help her care for Jeffrey and all she had to show for it was a string of screw-ups and bad luck. It was enough to make her want to cry.

And maybe she would. Once she was inside, maybe she'd shower off the club sweat and have a nice, long cry in bed. It wasn't the most cheerful of plans, but it was just about all she had the energy for.

She opened the door and stepped into her apartment. It was mostly quiet, broken only by the sound of her father's snoring from the couch. She carefully closed the door, not wanting to wake him up.

Just as the edge of the door met the frame, the door was pushed back against her. For a moment it made no sense; it was almost as if the door had exploded from its hinges and attacked her. It slammed back into her, slamming hard against her elbow and sending her stumbling back toward the kitchen counters. The counter slammed into her back hard and by the time she regained her footing, she saw why the door had behaved in such a way.

William Gault was rushing into the apartment. He'd apparently been outside, waiting for the moment she slipped into her apartment to attack. He came at her, hatchet raised, crossing her kitchen in long, lumbering strides.

With her back still aching, Ava felt panic try to overwhelm her. This was not just some sparring partner or a boxing match. This was a man with a hatchet, wanting very badly to kill her. She focused on that panic and used it as fuel as she instinctively delivered a hard jab. She was not fully on her feet so she did not get her full strength behind it, but it still did the job. The blow landed just below his neck, causing him to stagger a bit and make a gulping noise as he gasped for breath. He still brought the hatchet down, but she was able to duck away from the blow without a problem. From her sunken position, she delivered a brutal right hook to his ribs on the left side. He crumpled in that direction, leaning against the counter.

Ava reached into her purse for the gun but never got the chance to draw it out. Still gasping for air, Gault slashed out with the hatchet again. Ava leaned back, still pinned against the counter. The blow missed, but it was so close that she could feel the broken air of the motion on her nose as the blade missed her by about two inches.

She barely had time to register this before a third figure entered the kitchen. She didn't realize exactly what was happening until she saw the first punch delivered. By the time the new figure had thrown a second punch at Gault, she recognized not only the face, but the boxing stance of Roosevelt Burr. Her father had been stirred awake by the commotion and was coming to help. He had already landed two jabs and she watched as he drew back to deliver the left-handed uppercut that had won his so many matches.

"Dad, no!" she screamed. In her mind, she could not help but wonder…if her dad was out here to see what the commotion had been about, where was Jeffrey? How much longer before he came out to see what was going on?

She watched as her father worked Gault over—but Gault was faster. A fraction of a second before Roosevelt's next landed, Gault brought the hatchet out, slashing it out defensively. It was by sheer luck alone than the blade found purchase. Roosevelt screamed out as the blade tore through his shirt and the skin of his left shoulder. He staggered back, falling to the floor, but Gault seemed not to care. He wheeled back on Ava, again bringing the hatchet over his shoulder.

Something very similar to thunder sounded out in Ava's head in that moment. This man had killed four women in all. He would have killed five if he'd been luckier with Theresa Neilson. And now here he was, in her apartment—in *Clarence's apartment*—with her son just a few rooms away. Pure fury passed through her in that thunder, bringing a calm that was almost disarming.

Ava raised her right arm to ward off the blow. Gault's arm shuddered a bit and he drew it back again while also trying to push her back against the counter. When he pushed her, she caught his free arm and twisted it while also swinging her own body hard to the right, almost like she was trying to curl herself around him. The motion sent

Gault sailing into the kitchen counter (which seemed to be taken the brunt of the action) chest-first. When he hit the counter and rebounded lightly, Ava hammered two successive blows into his back, both directly along his left kidney.

Gault wailed and tried to turn to defend himself. When he did, he caught a jab to the face and another blow to his ribs. This blow was devastating, and Ava could feel ribs cracking under her fist. Gault howled again and finally dropped the hatchet. It clattered to the floor and he tried diving for it right away. When he did, Ava stopped him by bringing a knee up and striking him directly in the jaw.

Even Ava cringed at the noise of his jaw breaking and his teeth slamming together. When William Gault hit the floor, he was not moving. For a moment, Ava thought she'd killed the bastard, but she could just barely see the rise and fall of his back as he drew in breath.

She ignored him and rushed to her father's side. He was bleeding on the floor, and she couldn't tell how deep the cut was.

"How bad is it, Dad?"

"Deep, but too bad," he hissed. "Might wanna see if you can get the hospital on the line, I guess."

Ava nodded. Not having a telephone in the apartment, she would have to use the booth downstairs in the lobby. She grabbed her purse and handed her father the Model 10. "If he tries to move, shoot him in the knees."

He grinned despite his pain and said, "Honey, you just whooped his ass good. He's not getting up until the hospital folks lift him up on a stretcher."

Ava started for the door but her father's voice stopped her.

"Hey, Ava?"

"Yeah?"

She couldn't tell if the emotion in his face was from the pain or from the sentiment of what he said next.

"If that's how you carry yourself on the street…forget everything I ever said against you being a cop."

CHAPTER THIRTY FIVE

Frank did his best not to feel intimidated as he entered Minard's office. It was nothing new for Minard to call him in for a private conversation—especially not since tasking him with the guidance and care of Ava Gold. But today, Alvin Cunningham was also there, sitting across from Captain Minard. Cunningham was the chief of police and only bothered coming by the precinct when he needed a favor or when something had gone bad.

The look on his sour face made Frank think today was to handle some bad business.

"Chief Cunningham," Minard said, "this is Detective Frank Wimbly. He was the only detective to go to bat for Ava Gold and was with her for most of the events that transpired these last few days."

Skipping any sort of introduction, Cunningham looked directly at Frank and said, "So you were in on this insane sting operation she attempted to pull off last night?"

"Yes, sir, I was."

"And why did you agree to it?"

"Because she's good at the job," he said, the answer surprising him. "Even when she was getting it wrong on the hatchet killer case, she was still solving crimes. We got Tony Two and Little Johnny Jones in here, something that had never been pulled off before. And she discovered a shallow grave on Neibolt Street where—"

"I'm aware of what she's done," Cunningham said. "I'm also aware of how reckless, foolish, and big-headed it all was. Answer me this, Detective: do you think she's cut out for the job?"

Frank thought it over for a bit, eventually giving a stiff nod of his head. "Yes, sir. But she's had no training. She was tossed into this this because of her own arrogance as well as a misguided but brilliant attempt at positive PR for the department. And with no training, she *still* managed to get the killer."

"Some might argue the killer came right to her doorstep and she got lucky."

When Minard spoke up, it quite frankly shocked Frank. "With all due respect, Chief," Minard said, "William Gault's current doctors at the hospital might argue that her surviving the attack was much more than luck. She beat the hell out of him, and with expert precision.”

“I take all of this to mean that both of you would be in favor of keeping her on?”

“I would, yes sir,” Frank said.

Minard took a moment to answer. When he did, he chose each word slowly. “Half the damned city knows her name now. And she has connections to clubs and some of the more underground places that usually turn their noses up at the fuzz. Not to mention she took down two mobsters *and* got the hatchet killer.”

“So that’s a yes?” Cunningham asked sarcastically.

“Yes. But I would stipulate that she needs proper training.”

“If she stays on,” Cunningham said, getting to his feet, “I would expect Detective Wimbly to handle her training. For the start of it, if she looks bad…you look bad. Would you be open to that, Detective?”

He did not like the sound of it, but Frank nodded all the same. “Yes, sir.”

“Then have at it.”

He said nothing else. He simply gave them both looks of frustration and then walked out.

“He didn’t look too happy,” Frank said.

“Chief Cunningham isn’t the sort of man that is for gender equality,” Minard said. “He’s still peeved that I even gave her the job in the first place. I guarantee you he ignored all of what we just said, and is just thinking about the good publicity of keeping her on.”

“So…when are you going to tell her?” Frank asked.

“I was thinking now,” Minard said, grabbing for his phone.

***

Ava stared at Minard’s closed office door for a few moments before knocking. This was it. This was where he sent her home, considering her brief tenure with the NYPD a failed experiment. It had all just gone so poorly, it was the only reasonable assumption she could make. Gently, she finally knocked on the door. She had to use her left hand because there was a wrap on her right hand to keep the swelling down from all the punches she dished out the night before. “Can I come in, Captain?”

“Yes,” Minard called through the door. “Please come in.”

Ava entered and when she saw Frank was also there, she felt as if someone had nailed a coffin closed somewhere deep inside her heart.

170

"Have a seat," Minard said.

Ava did, trying not to seem too shaken. The last thing she wanted to do was get emotional in front of these two men. She'd take her lumps like every other officer who had sat in this chair and that would be the end of it.

"Gold," Minard said, "I have no choice but to remove you as an officer from the department. You understand, right?"

"Yes, sir," she said, not meeting his eyes.

"Good. Now, from this moment on, you will have the designation of *detective*."

Ava looked up to him as if he had just spoken to her in a different language. That closed coffin in her chest burst open as the realization of what he'd said sank over her. Surely, she'd misunderstood him.

"Sir?"

"Detective Gold. That's right," Minard said. Ava looked to Frank to see if they were having some sort of cruel joke at her expense. But all she saw was something that looked like a grin. Not a joke…but something close to joy or happiness.

"I want you to take the remainder of the week off to nurse those expert fists of yours," Minard said. "And when you come back, you will be running the detective beat with Detective Wimbly. Is that to your liking?"

The smile and the glistening of tears in her eyes could not be stopped. And in the end, she decided to just let them come. Weeping was quite different from showing genuine appreciation and gratitude, she supposed.

"Yes, sir," she said, as confidently as she could. "And you won't regret it."

Minard could not contain his chuckle when he said, "Oh, I suppose we'll have to see about that, won't we?" He then stood and, in a move that shocked Ava, he offered his hand to be shaken. "Enjoy your week off, Gold."

She shook with her uninjured hand and made her exit. She felt like she was floating rather than walking back to the WB offices. It felt like she was walking in a dream. She made her way slowly over to her desk, barely aware of the mail carrier passing through. She felt equal measures of gratitude and fear. She now had to really be on her game, had to make sure she was as professional as possible. And perhaps more than that, she had to keep in mind that people would definitely see Clarence through her now. She had to make him proud.

She sat down behind her desk and saw that the mail carrier had dropped a single letter off for her. It was a small envelope with her name written directly across the center. Ava opened the envelope and found a single sheet of paper inside. She took it out, unfolded it, and read it. The handwritten letter inside was very short. Still, it took her breath away and nearly made her drop the paper.

"What is it?" a soft voice asked from behind her; she knew it was Frances.

She handed the letter to Frances and as she read it, Ava recited it in her head: *Congrats, Ava! Looks like you're going to do well with this job. It's a shame that women aren't meant to be cops. If you're still here in a month, I'm going to make things SO HARD for you. Have fun playing make-believe while you can!*

"This has to be someone just messing with you." Frances tossed the letter back onto the desk as if it were a piece of garbage. "Some man jealous that a woman is getting the spotlight."

"Maybe," she said.

"If I were you, I'd show it to Captain Minard and get to the bottom of it."

"Yeah, that's a good idea," she said, getting to her feet. She hurried out of the WB office and back to the stairs. She hated to bother Minard so soon after leaving his office, but she thought this was important enough to do so.

She made her way back through the bullpen, to Minard's back office. His door was closed, so she raised her hand to knock. Just before she did, though, she heard Minard's voice inside, uttering a curse word. Another man spoke up and said: "I know, I know. But no one got there in time."

"That description sounds too damned familiar to me," Minard said. "One more time. What did the witness see?"

"A man in a workman's coat," the officer said. "Sort of short. Fired four shots and took off with a woman's purse."

"And the woman? I assume she's dead?"

"Not as of half an hour ago. She's barely hanging on in the hospital."

Ava did not need to hear any more. She walked away with the other officer's description in her head. *A man in a workman's coat. Sort of short.*

It was the exact description of the man who shot Clarence. She was sure it could be a coincidence, but who the hell wore a workman's coat in the dead of summer? She was certain it wasn't a coincidence. She was so certain that she exited the station, simply needing to get away for a while.

In the space of half an hour, she'd been giving an amazing opportunity, threatened by an insecure man via a short letter, and discovered that her husband's killer had attempted to kill again. It all made her feel as if the ceiling might collapse on her. She walked quickly outside and breathed the city air deep into her lungs to clear her mind.

Within just a few steps, she realized that she now had at least some degree of authority over these streets.

And in a city that only grew more and more each day, it was overwhelming in the absolute best way.

EPILOGUE

Ava was alarmed at how much she enjoyed the sight of Jeffrey in a boxing ring. He and another boy—the son of a man Roosevelt was training—were pretending to spar. She could already see where Jeffrey's footwork came naturally, even in pretending.

"I've seen him hit those bags," Roosevelt said, joining her at ringside. "If you allow it, I think he'd make a good boxer."

"I won't push him to it," she said. "And you better not, either. But I think he's going to end up loving it."

"Should I go ahead and get him some gloves for Christmas?" her father asked sarcastically.

"That would be pushing."

Roosevelt's left arm was in a sling. The gash to his supper chest had been quite deep and had required thirty-one stitches. The sling was to make sure he didn't act a fool at the gym and use the arm before the wound healed up properly.

"You know," Roosevelt said, "some of the guys are looking at you different now….now that you're a detective."

"How were they looking at me before?"

"As the wife of Clarence Gold. As the widowed daughter Roosevelt Burr. Now…well, now they're watching their manners because there's a detective on the premises."

"Good. Maybe it'll class the place up."

As they watched Jeffrey sparring, the front door opened. Ava was a bit surprised when Frank Wimbly came in. he looked around with a wide smile, taking in the sight and sounds of the place. When his eyes landed on Ava, he headed her way.

"Hey there, partner," Ava said with a smile. "Dad, this is my partner, Detective Frank Wimbly. Frank, this is—"

"Roosevelt Burr. I know. Good to meet you, sir. Big fan."

"Thanks," he said. Then, sensing business was in the air, he wandered away to where a student was struggling with a set of weights.

"What brings you here?" Ava asked.

"Well, there's a case that we need to get a start on. I wanted to meet up with you to go over the details before you're just tossed to the wolves."

"Another murder?"

"Nah, a robbery at Fellerman's Jewelry. Nothing dangerous it seems."

She nodded and, without looking at him, asked: "What's the attitude at the precinct like now that everyone knows I'm a homicide detective after less than a week?"

"Honestly, it's split down the middle. Some think it's a joke but there are some that are rooting for you."

She smiled and looked back to the ring where Jeffrey and the other boy had resorted to basic wrestling techniques, rolling around on the mat. Looking at him, she knew she *had* to be okay. Because taking this job had been more than just honoring Clarence in her own way. It was also about making sure this city was a safe place for her son to grow up. And as a mother and now a detective, if she could not do that, then why was she even trying?

She recited the last part of the letter she'd received yesterday, rolling it through her head as motivation.

If you're still here in a month, I'm going to make things SO HARD for you.

Her jaw set with anger as she watched Jeffrey at play, thinking.

Oh, I hope you do try, you son of a bitch...whoever you are. I truly hope you try.

CITY OF FEAR
(An Ava Gold Mystery—Book 2)

"A MASTERPIECE OF THRILLER AND MYSTERY. Blake Pierce did a magnificent job developing characters with a psychological side so well described that we feel inside their minds, follow their fears and cheer for their success. Full of twists, this book will keep you awake until the turn of the last page."
--Books and Movie Reviews, Roberto Mattos (re Once Gone)

CITY OF FEAR (An Ava Gold Mystery—Book 2) is a new novel in a long-anticipated new series by #1 bestseller and USA Today bestselling author Blake Pierce, whose bestseller Once Gone (a free download) has received over 1,000 five star reviews.

In the rough streets of 1920s New York City, 34 year-old Ava Gold, a widower and single mom, claws her way up to become the first female homicide detective in her NYPD precinct. She is as tough as they come, and willing to hold her own in a man's world.

When a 16-year-old girl from a wealthy Fifth Avenue family is found strangled, murdered on the eve of her society coming-out party, Ava, 1920s New York City's best female homicide detective, is called in to find the killer. She quickly learns that psychosis is pervasive even amongst the glamour of high society's wealthiest families.

Determined to find justice for the girl—and to stop the psychotic killer from killing again—Ava pries into the dangerous rings of powerful high society, finding herself threatened as she is singled out by a tycoon. Fighting for her job, trying to stop a killer, and finding herself in an unexpected romantic relationship, Ava finds herself in the battle of her life.

A heart-pounding suspense thriller filled with shocking twists, the authentic and atmospheric AVA GOLD MYSTERY SERIES is a riveting page-turner, endearing us to a strong and brilliant character that will capture your heart and keep you reading late into the night.

Book #3 in the series—CITY OF BONES—is now also available.

Blake Pierce

Blake Pierce is the USA Today bestselling author of the RILEY PAGE mystery series, which includes seventeen books. Blake Pierce is also the author of the MACKENZIE WHITE mystery series, comprising fourteen books; of the AVERY BLACK mystery series, comprising six books; of the KERI LOCKE mystery series, comprising five books; of the MAKING OF RILEY PAIGE mystery series, comprising six books; of the KATE WISE mystery series, comprising seven books; of the CHLOE FINE psychological suspense mystery, comprising six books; of the JESSIE HUNT psychological suspense thriller series, comprising nineteen books; of the AU PAIR psychological suspense thriller series, comprising three books; of the ZOE PRIME mystery series, comprising six books; of the ADELE SHARP mystery series, comprising thirteen books; of the EUROPEAN VOYAGE cozy mystery series, comprising six books (and counting); of the new LAURA FROST FBI suspense thriller, comprising five books (and counting); of the new ELLA DARK FBI suspense thriller, comprising six books (and counting); of the A YEAR IN EUROPE cozy mystery series, comprising nine books (and counting); of the AVA GOLD mystery series, comprising three books (and counting); and of the RACHEL GIFT mystery series, comprising three books (and counting).

An avid reader and lifelong fan of the mystery and thriller genres, Blake loves to hear from you, so please feel free to visit www.blakepierceauthor.com to learn more and stay in touch.

BOOKS BY BLAKE PIERCE

RACHEL GIFT MYSTERY SERIES
HER LAST WISH (Book #1)
HER LAST CHANCE (Book #2)
HER LAST HOPE (Book #3)

AVA GOLD MYSTERY SERIES
CITY OF PREY (Book #1)
CITY OF FEAR (Book #2)
CITY OF BONES (Book #3)

A YEAR IN EUROPE
A MURDER IN PARIS (Book #1)
DEATH IN FLORENCE (Book #2)
VENGEANCE IN VIENNA (Book #3)
A FATALITY IN SPAIN (Book #4)
SCANDAL IN LONDON (Book #5)
AN IMPOSTOR IN DUBLIN (Book #6)
SEDUCTION IN BORDEAUX (Book #7)
JEALOUSY IN SWITZERLAND (Book #8)
A DEBACLE IN PRAGUE (Book #9)

ELLA DARK FBI SUSPENSE THRILLER
GIRL, ALONE (Book #1)
GIRL, TAKEN (Book #2)
GIRL, HUNTED (Book #3)
GIRL, SILENCED (Book #4)
GIRL, VANISHED (Book 5)
GIRL ERASED (Book #6)

LAURA FROST FBI SUSPENSE THRILLER
ALREADY GONE (Book #1)
ALREADY SEEN (Book #2)
ALREADY TRAPPED (Book #3)
ALREADY MISSING (Book #4)
ALREADY DEAD (Book #5)

EUROPEAN VOYAGE COZY MYSTERY SERIES
MURDER (AND BAKLAVA) (Book #1)
DEATH (AND APPLE STRUDEL) (Book #2)

CRIME (AND LAGER) (Book #3)
MISFORTUNE (AND GOUDA) (Book #4)
CALAMITY (AND A DANISH) (Book #5)
MAYHEM (AND HERRING) (Book #6)

ADELE SHARP MYSTERY SERIES
LEFT TO DIE (Book #1)
LEFT TO RUN (Book #2)
LEFT TO HIDE (Book #3)
LEFT TO KILL (Book #4)
LEFT TO MURDER (Book #5)
LEFT TO ENVY (Book #6)
LEFT TO LAPSE (Book #7)
LEFT TO VANISH (Book #8)
LEFT TO HUNT (Book #9)
LEFT TO FEAR (Book #10)
LEFT TO PREY (Book #11)
LEFT TO LURE (Book #12)
LEFT TO CRAVE (Book #13)

THE AU PAIR SERIES
ALMOST GONE (Book#1)
ALMOST LOST (Book #2)
ALMOST DEAD (Book #3)

ZOE PRIME MYSTERY SERIES
FACE OF DEATH (Book#1)
FACE OF MURDER (Book #2)
FACE OF FEAR (Book #3)
FACE OF MADNESS (Book #4)
FACE OF FURY (Book #5)
FACE OF DARKNESS (Book #6)

A JESSIE HUNT PSYCHOLOGICAL SUSPENSE SERIES
THE PERFECT WIFE (Book #1)
THE PERFECT BLOCK (Book #2)
THE PERFECT HOUSE (Book #3)
THE PERFECT SMILE (Book #4)
THE PERFECT LIE (Book #5)
THE PERFECT LOOK (Book #6)
THE PERFECT AFFAIR (Book #7)

THE PERFECT ALIBI (Book #8)
THE PERFECT NEIGHBOR (Book #9)
THE PERFECT DISGUISE (Book #10)
THE PERFECT SECRET (Book #11)
THE PERFECT FAÇADE (Book #12)
THE PERFECT IMPRESSION (Book #13)
THE PERFECT DECEIT (Book #14)
THE PERFECT MISTRESS (Book #15)
THE PERFECT IMAGE (Book #16)
THE PERFECT VEIL (Book #17)
THE PERFECT INDISCRETION (Book #18)
THE PERFECT RUMOR (Book #19)

CHLOE FINE PSYCHOLOGICAL SUSPENSE SERIES
NEXT DOOR (Book #1)
A NEIGHBOR'S LIE (Book #2)
CUL DE SAC (Book #3)
SILENT NEIGHBOR (Book #4)
HOMECOMING (Book #5)
TINTED WINDOWS (Book #6)

KATE WISE MYSTERY SERIES
IF SHE KNEW (Book #1)
IF SHE SAW (Book #2)
IF SHE RAN (Book #3)
IF SHE HID (Book #4)
IF SHE FLED (Book #5)
IF SHE FEARED (Book #6)
IF SHE HEARD (Book #7)

THE MAKING OF RILEY PAIGE SERIES
WATCHING (Book #1)
WAITING (Book #2)
LURING (Book #3)
TAKING (Book #4)
STALKING (Book #5)
KILLING (Book #6)

RILEY PAIGE MYSTERY SERIES
ONCE GONE (Book #1)
ONCE TAKEN (Book #2)

ONCE CRAVED (Book #3)
ONCE LURED (Book #4)
ONCE HUNTED (Book #5)
ONCE PINED (Book #6)
ONCE FORSAKEN (Book #7)
ONCE COLD (Book #8)
ONCE STALKED (Book #9)
ONCE LOST (Book #10)
ONCE BURIED (Book #11)
ONCE BOUND (Book #12)
ONCE TRAPPED (Book #13)
ONCE DORMANT (Book #14)
ONCE SHUNNED (Book #15)
ONCE MISSED (Book #16)
ONCE CHOSEN (Book #17)

MACKENZIE WHITE MYSTERY SERIES
BEFORE HE KILLS (Book #1)
BEFORE HE SEES (Book #2)
BEFORE HE COVETS (Book #3)
BEFORE HE TAKES (Book #4)
BEFORE HE NEEDS (Book #5)
BEFORE HE FEELS (Book #6)
BEFORE HE SINS (Book #7)
BEFORE HE HUNTS (Book #8)
BEFORE HE PREYS (Book #9)
BEFORE HE LONGS (Book #10)
BEFORE HE LAPSES (Book #11)
BEFORE HE ENVIES (Book #12)
BEFORE HE STALKS (Book #13)
BEFORE HE HARMS (Book #14)

AVERY BLACK MYSTERY SERIES
CAUSE TO KILL (Book #1)
CAUSE TO RUN (Book #2)
CAUSE TO HIDE (Book #3)
CAUSE TO FEAR (Book #4)
CAUSE TO SAVE (Book #5)
CAUSE TO DREAD (Book #6)

KERI LOCKE MYSTERY SERIES

A TRACE OF DEATH (Book #1)
A TRACE OF MURDER (Book #2)
A TRACE OF VICE (Book #3)
A TRACE OF CRIME (Book #4)
A TRACE OF HOPE (Book #5)

www.ingramcontent.com/pod-product-compliance
Lightning Source LLC
Chambersburg PA
CBHW021659110726

47902CB00007B/1989